P9-CCK-956

"Silence, Berwyn!" bellowed Angarth the Dragon King.

Berwyn, the Dragon Queen, who was nearly as large and every bit as majestic as Angarth, hissed back a plume of steam.

This doesn't look good, Ethan thought worriedly. His friend Griffen, the loremaster, was missing, and now the two fiercest dragons in the realm were close to starting a war.

Angarth stared hard at Berwyn until she dropped seven pairs of lids down to veil her silvery eyes. "The loss of my loremaster is not a small matter," the Dragon King stated. "He was *stolen*."

"Griffen *stolen*?" Ethan cried, but his words were lost in the outcry that went up from the dragons gathered nearby.

"Impossible!"

"No one would dare!"

"Who would attempt such a thing?"

"Only another dragon," Angarth answered, advancing slowly on Berwyn. "The loremaster has been dragon-napped!"

To Franklin and Joe Marraffino

DRAGONFIRE

#3
The Curse Of Peredur

Morgana Rhys

PRICE STERN SLOAN
Los Angeles

Copyright © 1990 by Cloverdale Press, Inc.

Produced by Cloverdale Press, Inc.
96 Morton Street
New York, New York 10014

Published by Price Stern Sloan, Inc.
360 North La Cienega Boulevard
Los Angeles, California 90048

Printed in the United States of America. All rights reserved. No part
of this publication may be reproduced, stored in a retrieval system or
transmitted, in any form or by any means, electronic, mechanical,
photocopying, recording or otherwise, without the prior written per-
mission of the publishers.

ISBN: 0-8431-2717-1

10   9   8   7   6   5   4   3   2   1

One

Into the Woods

Halfway up the steep hill behind the house that overlooked Lords' Inlet, nine year old Ethan Lord stopped to catch his breath. Ahead of him his eleven year old stepbrother Nicholas danced up the bare rocky slope with the ease of a mountain goat.

"Hey, you guys!" Ethan's stepfather Thomas Lord yelled from the driveway directly below. Ethan turned around. Mr. Lord and Arnie Ducheyne were unloading a Christmas tree from the back of Arnie's blue pickup.

"What?" Ethan and Nicholas yelled back in unison.

Thomas Lord cupped his hands over his mouth like a megaphone. "I'll be in town at four o'clock sharp to pick you up. In front of the old curio shop on the corner of Breton Avenue. It's called Bangles and Bones. Don't be late or I'll trim the tree without you," he threatened playfully.

1

"Right," Ethan yelled back.

A stiff December wind whipped up from the choppy waters of the bay. Ethan pulled his blue stocking cap further down over his mop of longish blonde hair as he trudged along behind his brother. Behind his glasses his light-blue eyes were tearing from the cold.

"I thought you always had a white Christmas in Canada!" the nine year old grumbled in the general direction of Nicholas, who had already reached the crest of the hill where the pine woods started.

"We do — or did — until this year," Nicholas said in a way that made Ethan feel as if somehow an unwhite, plain brown and grey Christmas was his fault. Ethan's mother had married Nicholas's dad back in October and in the last couple of months the boys had more or less become pretty good friends. Still, Ethan hated being talked down to as if he were stupid and not just shorter and less athletic than Nicholas.

"But," Nicholas added, "If there really were lots of snow, Dad never would have let us hike across the woods down to Frenchman's Bay this afternoon to finish our Christmas shopping. The drifts in the woods here get high as — " Nicholas stopped and stretched his arm way above his head and winked. "High as a dragon's eye."

At the word "dragon" the glum expression

vanished from Ethan's face. He pushed up his glasses and grinned. "High as a Fingal dragon or a king dragon like Angarth or an old crusty sea wyrm like Drazyl?" Their last two visits to the Lord's family vacation home in Cape Breton, Nova Scotia, had landed the boys in the middle of some peculiar adventures involving dragons, an evil sorcerer and a cruel puppeteer with magical powers. Ever since, Ethan had been spending his free time at the library reading every book on dragons he could find. Nicholas, on the other hand, had done his best to pretend dragons didn't even exist. He was afraid of his friends in Boston making fun of him. Ethan was surprised that Nicholas brought the subject up now.

Nicholas pretended to consider Ethan's question. After checking that he was out of sight of the house and his stepmother, he pocketed his red earmuffs and ran his gloved fingers through his straight dark hair. Faking a local Cape Breton accent, he said with a frown. "Well — to tell the truth, eh. I think drifts only grow as big as a young dragon around here. Probably Fingal-size drifts, eh." He nodded sagely then strode into the dark pine forest.

Ten minutes later, Ethan's wish for a white Christmas came true. "Hey, it's started snowing!" he cried, and stuck his tongue out to taste the first few flakes.

"Looks like you've gotten your wish." Nicholas said, but when he glanced up to check the sky, he frowned. "Something strange is going on here. A minute ago the sky was blue, now it looks like a real storm's brewing."

Ethan followed Nicholas' gaze. Heavy grey clouds seemed to sag down beneath the trees. In the space of only a few minutes the flurries had changed to a dense icy snowfall. Ethan suddenly got scared. "You think it's all right to keep going? Maybe we should turn around before the storm gets worse."

"No way," scoffed Nicholas. "It's not that far to town. Twenty minutes and we'll be there."

"*If* we don't get lost!" Ethan grumbled. He thought a moment about turning back and heading home, but Nicholas would call him chicken. Besides, Ethan was more afraid of getting lost in the woods alone, than together with Nicholas. A moment later he stopped his trek up the slope. He knew what was happening. "Oh no," Ethan wailed suddenly above the rising wind.

Nicholas turned around at the noise. "You sound like a sick cat. What's wrong?"

"Nothing," replied Ethan, testily.

"So don't tell me." Nicholas gave a who-cares sort of shrug, then the wind gusted up so strong it pushed him back until he landed next to Ethan against a tree. "Hey, what's going on here?" Nicholas yelled up at the sky.

Ethan decided he'd better tell Nicholas. "I don't think this is an ordinary storm." He hemmed and hawed a moment, then forced himself to go on. "I think something strange is happening, you know, like when we ran into Fingal in the cave back in October, and like when our boat capsized in the bay last month and dumped us on the doorstep of Drazyl's kingdom beneath the sea. There were weird storms then too." Ethan stopped and waited for Nicholas to laugh.

Nicholas looked dead serious. Ethan's heart lurched right into his stomach and he felt a chill go up his spine.

Nicholas met Ethan's level gaze and stated flatly, "Someone's trying to lure us back to the Seven Kingdoms — aren't they?"

Ethan gave a timid nod. "I — I think so." The Seven Kingdoms was the name of the world where Ethan and Nicholas had had their adventures with dragons, first in the land of Nir, then in the desert reaches of Cynwyd.

For a long moment Nicholas said nothing. He slowly looked all around him. The blizzard had grown so bad, the forest looked the same in all directions: white with grey shadowy trees looming everywhere.

"Well it's Christmas Eve and they've got no right. I don't care who's in trouble this time,"

Nicholas said with force.

"Me neither," Ethan agreed. "So do we go back home?"

"No," Nicholas said uneasily. "We can't. I don't know how. I'm lost. Look." Nicholas took Ethan by the shoulders and turned him around. "There aren't even any tracks. I think we should go to our left. But there's a hill there I don't remember."

Sure enough, through the thick snowfall Ethan could see that the ground went up. The house on Lords' Inlet should be downhill from where they were standing. But everywhere Ethan looked, the trees seemed to march upward through the forest.

"Standing here's not helping a thing," Nicholas said firmly. "I say we should go that way," he pointed straight ahead. "The hill's less steep, and the wind will be at our back. Up top we might be able to see where we are."

"Not unless this blizzard stops," Ethan murmured as they started trudging, but the wind drowned out his words.

Nicholas reached the crest first. The down side of the hill was steep but bare of trees. Nicholas stared hard through the curtain of flakes. To his dismay an even higher heavily forested ridge lay just across the way. A sea of mist swirled up toward him from the hollow, and a soft but steady hiss filled the air.

Ethan dropped his voice to a whisper and asked. "What's that sound?"

Nicholas started to shrug, then stepped forward a little to hear better. The snow was even slipperier than it looked. Nicholas's arms flayed out as he tried to keep his balance. Instinctively, Ethan grabbed his hand. But Nicholas weighed more and pulled Ethan down on the icy surface with him. The two boys slid down the hill, yelling at the top of their lungs. Their fall ended in a mist-shrouded glen.

The hissing ceased, as if the forest had caught its breath.

Nicholas reached for Ethan as they skidded to a stop, his mouth wide open. For in front of them loomed a huge, jagged shape, the size of a small house.

Then a spicy apple-pie sort of scent wafted from the heart of the glen right to Ethan's nose. He gave a cautious quiet sniff. It was a familiar, friendly smell. He sniffed again, and a huge grin spread across his face. Before Nicholas knew what was happening, Ethan bolted free of his grip, straight into the glen.

Two

Encounters of a Friendly Kind

"Ethan!" Nicholas screamed in horror at the very same moment Ethan shouted with joy, "Fingal! It's you! It's you!"

Nicholas plunged through the curtain of mist and stopped short at the sight that met his eyes. A smallish purple-green dragon sat on one side of the clearing by the side of a frozen pond. The creature had melted a hole in the ice and was calmly sitting on the shore, fishing. His pole was a birch sapling; his line, a length of twisted vine. An impressive stack of trout shimmered on a rock beside him. Ethan was standing by the dragon's coiled tail, hungrily eyeing the fish.

Fingal beamed and gave his fishing rod a shake. "Welcome to the Gates of Peredur," he said.

"Peredur in the Northern Reaches?" Nicholas squawked, and Ethan blinked with surprise.

9

"How do you know about Peredur?" Ethan asked.

"Maps, toadbrain. Maps I saw in Breton's study in Nir when I was pretending to be his apprentice."

Nicholas was cold and hungry, and it occurred to him that landing in the Seven Kingdoms on Christmas Eve was a pretty rotten trick. "Why'd you make us go through all this?" he asked the dragon. "If you wanted to find us, you could have met us right back there in the woods. We've been walking for miles and we're cold and — "

Fingal looked very guilty, and propped his fishing rod on a rock. "I am sorry. I blew up that storm because I thought you might enjoy it. I forget humans get cold in the snow." Using his claws, he scraped together a pile of twigs and branches. Two puffs of his dragon breath, and the heap began to smolder. A moment later it blazed into a roaring fire.

"But why did you bring us here?" Ethan asked, stepping forward to warm his hands.

Fingal sighed and one of his eyes whirled purple, the other a pale, troubled blue. "You are not happy to see me, are you?"

"Well," Nicholas said, trying not to hurt Fingal's feelings. "Your timing, it sort of — stinks."

Nicholas was so blunt, Ethan gulped. By

10

dragon standards Fingal was very young. Still, even with a teenage dragon it paid to be polite. "What Nicholas means is, couldn't you have *asked* us first if we wanted to come to Peredur? Or let us plan ahead?"

"There is no time to plan ahead," said Fingal. "Not when all of the Seven Kingdoms is on the brink of war."

"War?" the boys echoed.

"What can we do about a war?" asked Nicholas, who never shied away from a fistfight but had recently signed a nationwide petition against war of any sort.

"Sssshhhhh." The dragon swiveled his long neck around and squinted into the darkening forest behind him. "Spies," he hissed softly. "There may be spies."

The dragon, Ethan and Nicholas all held their breath. The only sounds were the distant hoot of an owl, the creak of treetops in the wind and the crackle of their own small fire.

"No one's listening," Nicholas said finally. "But I'll tell you right now, we aren't going to get involved. And what's all this talk about spies?"

"I can't tell you that," Fingal said in dismay. "I brought you to this forest because I want you to choose. To stay or to leave. You've already been called to the Seven Kingdoms twice. You have proven beyond a doubt you are both heroes.

But this time, the task is more difficult. A battle looms that might determine the future of all dragons." Fingal shivered, rattling his scales. "You can stay here and help, or I can send you back."

"Now?" Ethan's eyes widened. The moon was rising, he noticed, and he knew that if they chose to go back home, it would still be early afternoon in the "real world."

"Now," said Fingal sadly. "If you want me to. But I would like to tell you why I called you here first."

"That's only fair," Nicholas agreed. Even as he spoke, Nicholas got a funny feeling that Fingal was playing a trick. Not a dirty trick, but a dragon sort of trick. Nicholas took a deep breath and wondered if Ethan had figured it out yet. Fingal's story, whatever it was, would probably make them *want* to stay.

"Good." Fingal lowered several pairs of lids over his eyes and for a moment appeared to be thinking. Then he began, "I only know pieces of the truth. There are forces at work — very powerful forces — that want to keep the truth hidden. Usually, dragons have the gift of letting their minds touch. I can be many miles from other dragons, but if I am very still, I can hear what other dragons are saying or thinking. Of course," Fingal added quickly, "we are very polite about this, and do not listen in unless we let other dragons know we plan to do so."

"Like telephones," Ethan nodded, very impressed.

"Yeah," Nicholas said, not sure he believed Fingal. "So then why don't you know what's really going on?"

"Because now a dragon — or someone — with powers much greater than mine has blocked our lines of communication.

Nicholas bit his lower lip. "If these forces are so strong, what can we do that you can't? We're just kids."

"You are heroes from another place in time. Magic spells in the Seven Kingdoms don't seem to hold you as long. Some spells don't even work on you. No one seems to know why . . . . You come from a place with different laws, I think. Besides," Fingal paused ever so slightly. "Olwyn needs you."

"Olwyn's in trouble?" said Nicholas, leaping to his feet. Standing up, he still came only chest high to the seated dragon, but he looked up and locked his glance with the beast's. "Why didn't you say that to begin with? There's no question we'll help her, and you know it."

"No matter how long it takes," Ethan said. "No matter what we have to do. Olwyn's our friend."

"Do not be hasty with this decision." Fingal's

quiet warning surprised them. To Nicholas there was nothing that could stand in the way of helping Olwyn, the lovely, headstrong daughter of Griffen, Nir's Loremaster.

"We promised her we'd come back and help her find her father," Ethan said softly. "We would have stayed with her in Cynwyd if we could have."

"There was no choice," Fingal reminded Ethan. "The sea dragon had promised to send you home if you kept your end of the bargain. He had to keep that promise or everything would have returned to the way it was before you entered his kingdom. Besides, dragons *always* keep their word."

"But what's happening to Olwyn?" Nicholas asked. "Has she found Griffen and Nir's lost king?"

"Did she send you to find us?" Ethan added.

Fingal threw up his front paws. "One question at a time. No, Olwyn did not send me to find you. She doesn't know I have come for you. She does not even know how much danger she's in. She only knows that her father traveled as far as the borders of Peredur. Then vanished."

"Into thin air?" Nicholas was skeptical. He sensed Fingal was leaving something out. An important clue.

"Yessss" Fingal hedged. "And no. Griffen was last seen with Angarth. When you two returned to Cape Breton from Nir, Griffen and Angarth set out to find Kryspyn, Nir's rightful king. And for a long time, messages from dragons in the west and Northern Reaches mentioned Angarth and his honored loremaster companion. Then, several weeks ago, just before your journey to the castle beneath the sea, the channels broke down."

"Several weeks ago," Nicholas mused, piecing together bits of Fingal's story. "That was just about when Olwyn began dreaming her father was in some kind of trouble."

"Yes," Fingal said, and Nicholas was sure the young dragon was hedging again. "Of course there have been rumors. The latest is that Angarth no longer has him."

Ethan asked, "Who's spreading rumors?"

"Dragons," Fingal replied promptly.

"And what else does this dragon hotline say?" Nicholas was getting impatient.

"Nothing," responded Fingal.

"Come off it, Fingal," Nicholas snapped. "Stop playing games. There's something you are not telling us. Why?"

"Because I do not know the truth — it is hidden. This is why coming here for you is very dangerous. This is dragon business, and I should not ask humans to help. But Olwyn is your friend. So, I must give you a choice: to stay and help, or leave — before it is too late."

"Why is this quest more dangerous than the others back in Nir or Cynwyd?" Ethan asked in a shaky voice.

"Because this time there is trouble between dragons."

Ethan twirled the long stocking of his blue cap a moment, then looked directly at Fingal and managed a weak smile. "But there really is no choice. You know that."

Fingal shuffled uncomfortably, and turned his face from the firelight.

"We've got to help Olwyn, no matter what," Nicholas said.

"Then first thing in the morning I will bring you to her," the dragon said quickly. "She will not be expecting you. And you must not tell her about the dragons or that I brought you here. I have broken many dragon rules telling you even this much. No one must know I sent for you."

Fingal then spread his wings. Their iridescence glistened in the moonlight. "I will keep you warm while you rest," he offered. Nicholas crept under his left wing; Ethan his right. Gently the beast folded his wings over them like a tent. Warmth poured out of the dragon's body, as if it were a woodburning stove, and the boys nestled closer to him. His spicy scent enveloped them. Gradually the low purr-like hum rumbling from deep down inside the dragon's chest lulled the boys to sleep.

It seemed he had only just closed his eyes when Nicholas felt himself shaken awake.

"You sleep too late!" Fingal said, and shook his scales. He prodded Nicholas in the back. "You must wake up. Now." Then the dragon shuffled off and Nicholas heard a splash.

"Ummmm," Nicholas mumbled, still convinced it was the middle of the night. He looked straight up. Overhead the stars were gone, and the pale blue sky was bright with clear morning light.

"It's tomorrow already?" Nicholas murmured, rubbing the sleep from his eyes.

"Fingal wants to set out right after his bath," Ethan said.

"Bath?" Nicholas propped himself up on his elbow and his eyes widened. The dragon was sporting in the middle of the icy pond. Nicholas shivered just to watch.

The dragon caught Nicholas's eye and waved a friendly talon in his direction. "We can set out now. Olwyn is waiting, though she does not know it. We must find her before she goes beyond the town of Peredur into the Northern Reaches."

Three

Peredur and the Dragon Queen

"We're here." Fingal's breath rose in steamy clouds, then sailed out over the valley below. All morning he and the boys had trekked through the forest and up the steep snowy slopes to Peredur. As they marched, he had blazed a trail before them, melting the snow with his fiery breath.

Across the clearing from where the two boys stood, ice capped peaks towered high into the clouds. Scattered farmsteads dotted the narrow valley below. To the left, nestled in the foot of the craggy mountains, was a small town.

Fingal stretched out one claw in the direction of the village. "That's Peredur," he said. "There's an inn there. You can find your way easily from here. The snow is not as deep in the valley. You won't need my help to get through the drifts. Besides I cannot travel farther with

18

you. I've already interfered too much in this dragon feud."

Nicholas breathed an exasperated sigh. But Ethan cut him off. "At least you can show us where Olwyn is," he said.

"Beneath the sign of the Dragon Queen," replied Fingal with a cryptic smile. Slowly, he flapped his wings to warm up for flight. The boys ducked as he took to the air. He circled them once, then soared high over their heads and out of sight.

"He's the one who brought us here to help," Nicholas grumbled. "He could have been a little more helpful."

Ethan shrugged. "Standing here being upset with Fingal won't do us any good. Besides, didn't he say there was some kind of inn in Peredur? Inns in stories always have fires and lots of good food." Ethan shivered and patted his stomach. "I'm cold and hungry. If we're starving and half-frozen, we won't be any help to Olwyn."

"*If* we find her," Nicholas muttered.

As Fingal had predicted, their climb down from the hill was fairly easy. Within the hour they found themselves on the outskirts of the tiny hamlet. From the top of the hill, the snow-covered farmyards had looked neat and well tended. Up close the boys were startled to find the barn doors flung open and the houses deserted. Piles of dirt and rocks, some big as boulders, blocked the cobbled road.

"Looks like a ghost town to me," Nicholas said with a frown. They had reached a small cluster of houses around the town square. Carefully, he picked his way around the rubble and fallen trees. "I bet no one's lived here for years."

Ethan shook his head. "It doesn't feel like that. It feels like whoever was here left in a hurry and not very long ago. Look," he added "nothing in that blacksmith's shop is rusty yet, and everything is lying around."

Nicholas followed the direction of Ethan's gaze. The fire was out in the smithy's forge. A half-flattened horseshoe dangled from a pair of tongs balanced on the low wall around the fire pit.

Across the square from the smith was a two-story building, set well back from the street. Over the arched entrance a wooden sign squeaked in the wind. The letters were faded, but Nicholas could still make them out: THE DRAGON QUEEN. Below the words was a drawing of a dragon wearing a strand of pearls around its neck.

"This is the place," Nicholas said. Without waiting for Ethan, he marched through the gateway. The stable door was open, the stalls empty.

"Ethan," Nicholas called back over his shoulder. "I'm not sure Olwyn's still here."

Ethan came running after Nicholas. "I don't think *anyone*'s here at all. Not in the whole town," he added breathlessly.

"Well maybe since they all left so fast, they left some food," Nicholas said, and opened the broad plank door to the inn.

It took a moment to get used to the dark. It was a minute more before the boys realized the entrance hall was warm — or at least not as cold as the world outside. Instinctively, Ethan lowered his voice. "Someone's here. Or somewhere close nearby."

Nicholas went on ahead of his brother. The entrance hall quickly widened into a large common room. An enormous hearth filled half the far wall, and a fire blazed beneath an iron kettle. Seated in a corner near the blackened stones of the fireplace was a cloaked and hooded figure.

The brothers exchanged glances. Nicholas summoned his courage and cleared his throat. The sound rang out in the empty room. Slowly the figure turned. The movement made its hood fall back, and a cascade of dark blonde hair tumbled out. It was a girl, who looked at them with astonished blue eyes.

"Olwyn," Nicholas shouted, and crossed the room in two long strides. He grabbed her thin

21

hands and pulled her to her feet.

"We found you," Ethan cheered, and skipped up and planted a friendly kiss on Olwyn's cheek.

Olwyn smiled but seemed too shocked to speak.

"Beneath the Sign of the Dragon," Ethan chuckled. "He tricked us. He knew exactly where you'd be."

Nicholas turned away from Olwyn. "Shut up," he hissed under his breath.

Ethan winced. He had forgotten he wasn't supposed to mention Fingal to the girl. Then he spoke up quickly, hoping Olwyn hadn't noticed his slip. "Are you surprised to see us?"

Olwyn pulled up two stools and the boys sat down. "How'd you ever find me here?" she asked as she shrugged her cape off. She was wearing loose soft leggings, a boy's jerkin and a slender dagger at her belt. Smiling, she reached for two more mugs and ladled a steamy chocolatey-smelling brew from the kettle on the hearth and handed each boy a cup.

"You *were* supposed to call if you needed us," Nicholas reminded her sharply.

"I — I don't exactly need you," Olwyn hesitated, not meeting his gaze. "I mean, I'm glad to see you, but nothing's changed much since you were here last."

"You haven't found your father." Nicholas

said, careful not to let his voice betray him. Fingal had warned them not to let Olwyn know that her father was no longer with Angarth.

Olwyn shook back her hair from her face. It shone like gold in the firelight. "I don't know where to start. You two vanished with Drazyl and I went back to Cynwyd. A day or two later I joined a band of traders traveling north. One of them had actually seen Angarth and my father only a few weeks before, heading for these Northern Reaches." She paused and let out a deep sigh.

"They never made it this far. I'm sure of that. Once I got within five leagues of here, all the stories about my father stopped. No one from Peredur — that is, when there were still people in Peredur — had seen him, or even heard of him. Everyone had heard of Angarth though, but when I asked where he was, people got very quiet very fast. The only dragon they mention by name is a Queen Dragon called Berwyn."

"I didn't know there were girl dragons."

Olwyn withered Ethan with a look.

"How come we've never seen any?" Nicholas asked. "Or even *heard* of them until now?"

Olwyn blew into her mug before answering. "Because they prefer the cold of the Northern Reaches, for one thing. And because most of the dragons you've met up until now have been guardians of the portals of time. Male dragons rule time and space. Females, the earth and air. You've also met Angarth. He's a king, whose powers rule all the earth and fire and air and space and time and water. The same powers Berwyn has, because she's a queen," she hastened to add with an indignant sniff.

"What do people say about Berwyn?" Ethan asked.

"Not much — but enough," Olwyn answered. "She's the reason there are no people in Peredur. So I haven't had a chance to find out too much about her. But last night before the innkeeper left, he told me Berwyn could uproot the mountains. I didn't believe him — "

"But you do now," Nicholas stated.

Olwyn nodded. "The only other thing the innkeeper told me is that Berwyn is enraged at someone — or something. The strange part is that I usually can sense at least some of the sendings of the dragons. I can't get deep into their thoughts — ever — though my father sometimes can, when he is permitted. But now, I sense only lots of confusion and anger. I wonder if Berwyn is strong enough to block the channels of sending."

Ethan and Nicholas exchanged glances. Fingal had been telling the truth then. The dragon hot line was down. But Fingal hadn't mentioned Berwyn.

24

Meanwhile, Olwyn was still talking about Berwyn. "She's in such a fury, she's been shaking the earth. People have been driven from their homes. Last night I thought the walls of this place would cave in. The innkeeper thought so too. That's why he left."

"A dragon that shakes the earth?" Ethan chuckled. "You mean there was an earthquake," he went on a bit scornfully. "Dragons don't cause earthquakes, The movement of tectonic plates — "

"What kind of plates?" Olwyn asked looking down at the pewter mug she held.

"Don't pay attention to him," Nicholas said. "Brainwave here is about to give you a science lecture about how the continents were formed, and cracks beneath the surface of the earth." Turning to Ethan, Nicholas commented sharply, "Showing off right now is pretty stupid. Griffen's still lost, and we're wasting a lot of time talking in range of a very angry dragon."

"So, do you have any idea how we'll find your father?" Ethan asked, trying to ignore Nicholas.

Olwyn's face lit up with a smile. "So you'll help me, even though I didn't call for you?"

"Why else would we be here?" Ethan winked.

"I'm not sure," Olwyn said carefully. "There's a lot you're not telling me. But I'm not a loremaster's daughter for nothing. You probably have a reason for your secrets, and

I'll respect that."

Nicholas stood up and began to search the room. Opening a tall, wooden cupboard, he gathered together some old bread and cheese. It might not taste good, but they didn't have much choice. "The trail to your father led you this far. Which way does your loremaster's instinct tell you we should go from here?"

Olwyn threw up her hands. "I don't know. It's as if someone is jumbling the messages I get even in my dreams. Some very powerful force is at work. I am sure — almost — " she faltered slightly, then forced herself to go on. "He *is* alive. But something else inside says I should find Berwyn."

"Go *look for* this crazy Queen Dragon?" Ethan asked.

"Are you sure, Olwyn?" Nicholas tried to sound brave. "Looking for your father seems more important."

Olwyn pressed her fingers to her temples and squeezed her eyes shut. "I know, I know," she whispered. "But I can't help but feel my father's fate is tangled with the Dragon Queen." She looked up and seemed a little embarrassed. "Berwyn — I've never met her, or barely heard of her in the lore, yet I feel as if she is not just angry — it's as if she's in pain." Her eyes when she looked at the boys pleaded for them to understand. "I need to help her."

Four

Buried Alive

The next morning before they left the inn, Olwyn rummaged through the innkeeper's quarters. There, in a battered sea chest, she found clothes for the boys: fur-lined capes and tunics and extra squares of sturdy cotton cloth to use for carrying bundles.

"I'm not sure what trouble lies ahead," she said when the boys had changed, "but we'd better be wary of any strangers. If anyone asks, we're traders from Nir." She stepped back and gave Ethan, then Nicholas a critical look. "Good, you can still pass as apprentices of some sort. I'll just be myself — an apprentice loremaster, except no one must know I'm Griffen's daughter. Fortunately around here no one knows Griffen by sight, though some people have heard of him. I'll say I'm from Cynwyd." She pointed to the deeply dyed silk shirt she wore beneath her cape. Cynwyd was famous throughout the Seven Kingdoms for its dyed

27

goods. "If my father is in danger, my presence in Peredur might just cause more trouble."

They downed a quick breakfast of the stale bread and cheese, then they packed up more food and left the inn. Outside, stars still dotted the dawn sky. Olwyn stopped for a moment and looked up and down the dark street.

"Which way are we going?" Ethan asked. "You said the trail ends here."

"It does." Olwyn bit her lip and pulled her hood up over her hair. "I have no idea which way my father went. But I still have this feeling I must seek out Berwyn. She lives in the Northernmost Reaches. So we'll go north." Olwyn paused to get her bearings then started up the road, carefully picking her way in the dim light.

Their progress was slow, but by the time the sun shone above the trees, Nicholas figured they had gone at least five miles.

Olwyn suddenly stopped at a sharp bend in the road. "I've seen this place before," she whispered. She turned around and looked at Nicholas, her blue eyes frightened. "Remember that dream I had, before I met you on the way to Cynwyd?"

"The one where your father called for help?" Nicholas said. How could he forget it. In Olwyn's dream her father had told her to summon the boys back from Cape Breton.

"This is the place where I saw him. The exact spot. I remember those three jagged rocks and the trees." She motioned toward a stand of tall pines. "It wasn't winter then but there was snow, and it was cold like it is now. A dark cloud swept across the sky, and blanked out everything but my father's voice calling me."

Hearing Olwyn's story made Ethan shiver. He wrapped his fur cloak more tightly around him. A loud rumble from somewhere overhead made him look up. "Isn't that funny," he said, "thunder on a sunny winter day."

"Thunder?" Nicholas began to scoff, then heard the noise himself. A second later he screamed. "Avalanche!" He started to point to the massive peak towering just above them. An enormous sheet of snow was plunging through the trees. Instinctively, Nicholas reached for Ethan and threw Olwyn to the ground, trying to shield them both with his body. "Airholes," he cried, "We've got to make a pocket of air — " The rest of his words were choked off.

It felt like a wet blanket had landed on his back. Except the blanket was sharp and dug into him. As suddenly as the thunder of the avalanche had started, it stopped. There was another sound now. Something panting, and then the familiar beat of large wings. Nicholas should have been cold, but he was warm. Not

just warm, but actually sweating inside his Peredur-style coat.

"It is finished. You can look now," said a friendly, very familiar voice.

"Fingal!" Ethan recognized it first. He squirmed out from beneath Nicholas and sat up. His glasses were tilted on his nose and his hand was bruised from where it had pressed against a rock. He felt his arms and legs and flexed his toes. "Where in the world did you come from?"

"The sky," Fingal said simply. "I was flying by and I heard the evil noise. I looked and saw the three of you. It looked as if you needed a shield." He looked fondly at Ethan, then favored Nicholas with a sheepish sort of smile and bowed slightly to Olwyn.

Olwyn narrowed her eyes. "You just *happened* to be flying by," she said slowly. "At the exact moment Berwyn was having a temper tantrum."

At the sound of Berwyn's name, Fingal's hackles rose. He shuddered visibly and cast a nervous glance over his huge shoulder. "Berwyn is angry?" Fingal said in a shaky voice. "I didn't know she was involved in all this."

"You must be the one dragon in the Seven Kingdoms who hasn't heard about Berwyn being on the rampage. And what do you mean about 'all this'?" Olwyn asked sharply. "If I didn't know you couldn't lie, I'd swear you were trying to hide something from me." She waited a moment, then planted her hands on her hips. "Well, are you?" she asked.

Fingal shot the boys an appealing glance.

Right, Ethan thought. *Since dragons can't lie, either Nicholas or I have to cover for him.* Quickly, he said "We haven't seen Fingal for a while now." It was almost the truth. A while could mean a year, a month, even a day or just overnight.

"Olwyn," Nicholas cried out from a little ways up the road. "Look at this!" He half-walked, half-skidded down toward her. A silver pendant dangled from the leather thong in his hand.

"It's my father's." Olwyn said, taking the pendant from Nicholas. "He would never part with this. Not while he's alive." It took a moment for her words to sink in.

Nicholas stared dumbly at Olwyn and wished he had never found the pendant hanging on the tree.

Ethan shook out his cap then settled it back on his head. He stared at the silver claw, then at the white-faced Olwyn. Finally he looked at the bush where Nicholas had found the Loremaster's token. "He's not dead," Ethan stated flatly and looked at his friends. Three surprised faces looked back at him. "The avalanche cleared the road up ahead. It cleared away the snow from the trees. There's no sign of your father, but this claw has been buried in the snow for days at least. Look at it."

Olwyn examined the pendant carefully. Sure enough, the strip of leather was already rotting away. As if it had been lying beneath the snow for weeks. "But how did it get here?" she asked, her voice filled with relief.

Nicholas had ventured farther up the trail. "I've got an idea," he called. "Maybe we were supposed to find it." The road was rough and steep but it was broad. As he walked, Nicholas scanned every inch of ground and looked at each bush. Soon his search payed off. "I found something else. Griffen's whistle."

Fingal flew up the road, and settled close to Nicholas. He narrowed his eyes and sniffed the air. "There are more things, nearby, that smell of the Loremaster." He slapped one of the stunted trees with his wing tips. A flute fell out of its branches. In a few minutes they had located Griffen's embroidered belt and a dragon ring he used to wear on his left hand. "But the smell is old," the dragon added. "As if he passed this way one, two, maybe even four, days ago."

"You realize what's happening," Olwyn exclaimed. "He dropped these things on purpose. He's left a trail for us to follow. Though

33

I don't know why he left all this stuff so close together."

"So he's not only alive, but he's well enough to outwit whoever's captured him," Nicholas said without thinking.

Fingal grunted and started to cough. Great swirls of ashy smoke bellowed out of his mouth and threatened to smother the small group of travelers. For the next few minutes they forgot all about Griffen and concentrated on merely breathing.

But Olwyn wasn't fooled. "What's this about him being captured?" she asked as soon as she stopped coughing.

"To be honest," Ethan began, casting an apologetic look at Fingal.

Seven pairs of lids slammed shut on the young dragon's eyes. "Doomed," the young beast muttered and hunkered down on the snow with a sigh. "I am doomed."

Ethan went on anyway. "I'm sure something's happened to your father, or he wouldn't have to leave a trail. Maybe he got lost. Maybe he's not captured. Maybe he just wants to be sure someone can find him, and follow after him in case he runs into serious trouble. After all, he was off looking for the king."

"And maybe," Nicholas said, pointing a little ways up the road, "he and Angarth had to part

34

company. There where the road forks."

Fingal's eyes opened, and he glanced up at the sun. It was just overhead. "I cannot stay here," he said abruptly. "I am very late." With that he began to circle the ground, trying to clear a wide enough swatch for take off.

"Hold it!" Nicholas grabbed onto one of his wings. "You're not going anywhere just yet. Why don't you use that keen dragon nose of yours and smell which road the loremaster went down. You'll save us time."

Fingal breathed out a smoky sigh. "I cannot tell you what road. I cannot smell the road — that is part of — " he hesitated and added with great reluctance, "the magic that is at work."

"The dragon channels are closed to you, too?" Olwyn gasped.

"Yesss," Fingal said. "But I can tell you that there are two roads. You must make your choice and continue to search. But I cannot stay here. I am overdue at Dragon moot."

Olwyn's head snapped up. "Dragon moot? Who called this moot?" she demanded to know.

Fingal drew himself up tall and suddenly looked quite imposing for a not quite grown-up dragon. "I cannot say that."

Olwyn looked chastened. "No, of course not. But now I'm more worried than ever. News of a Dragon moot is never good."

"What exactly is a Dragon moot?" asked Ethan.

"A gathering of dragons — all dragons," explained Olwyn. "Usually because there is some kind of problem. But more than that, I just don't know. I'm not yet learned in that part of the lore."

"Did you say *all* dragons?" Nicholas suddenly asked. "That means Angarth will be there — "

"And maybe my father." Olwyn started to laugh. "So if we come with you to the moot then we — "

"You cannot come with me to the moot," Fingal declared firmly.

"But if Angarth has brought my father — "

Nicholas didn't let Olwyn continue. He shook her shoulder and forced her to face him. "We don't know that. We only know your father left a trail and that he may not be with Angarth. If we *all* go to the moot together and Griffen's not there, we'll have wasted too much time. We'll have to backtrack to here, and by then if he went down the other fork in the road, his trail would really be cold."

Olwyn fingered the dragon claw pendant. "So we should split up here. I wonder though if there *will* be more of a trail. How much more stuff did he have to leave behind?"

Fingal cleared his throat. "I have a plan." He

36

visibly gulped then went on. "I will probably get in trouble for this, but I will take one of you to the moot in case Griffen turns up. I doubt he will. I cannot promise even Angarth will be there, but if he is, he will surely remember Ethan from Nir. After all, it was Ethan who convinced him to help defeat the sorcerer. They spent a lot of time together. He likes Ethan."

"You want me to go to a Dragon moot? With you?" Ethan squeaked, casting a desperate glance in Nicholas's direction. "What happens to people at a moot who — uh — don't belong there?"

Fingal grumbled and mumbled in dragon-speak, so low, that Ethan could barely hear. "*Urthfydingydropoff.*"

"That sounds awful," Ethan commented with a gulp. "Doesn't it?" He looked toward Nicholas. He didn't want to risk being urthfydingydropoffed, whatever that might be, without Nicholas around to try at least to rescue him.

Nicholas rocked back and forth on his heels a moment before replying. "Fingal's right. One of us should go to the moot. On the way, you can check out the road to see if Griffen left any more signs. We'll take the other road that leads up toward those mountains. Between the four of us — "

Ethan had been listening carefully. "So

37

there's no choice then."

Nicholas looked down at him. "I don't like to split up either, but Fingal already explained, you *have* to go."

"Yes," Ethan said softly. "I guess I do." He straightened his shoulders. "I'll do it then."

"Good!" Nicholas clapped him on the back.

"It's our best chance," Olwyn agreed, shouldering her lute. "Now, let's get going, before the light fails. Once it's dark, we'll miss any clues my father might have left." She turned toward Fingal. "Do you know where this road leads?"

"The right road leads to the Northernmost Reaches. The dwellings of the mothers." At the confused looks on the boys' faces, Fingal explained. "That is the name we give the female dragons. They are the mothers and source of us all. They will all be at the moot too. Our road," he said to Ethan, "leads down to a flat, high place that overlooks the Valley of the Lost Dragon."

Nicholas handed Ethan his bundle and shouldered his own pack. "Good luck, kid," he said, then jauntily set off down the right fork behind Olwyn.

Ethan watched them with a sinking heart. He wanted to do his part to help find the loremaster, but he wanted to do it together with Nicholas, not alone.

Silently, Fingal spread his wings, inviting Ethan to climb on his back. The dragon took to the air, but flew low over the gently curving road that led down to the Valley of the Lost Dragon, trying to pick out Griffen's track.

Five

Masked Intruder

"No sign of Griffen. None at all," Ethan said with a sigh several hours later. He sank wearily onto a tree stump and flexed his aching feet.

The nearer they got to the Dragon moot, the more reluctant Fingal was to fly. At the moment, Ethan wished Fingal weren't so afraid of being seen by other dragons. It was only a matter of time before they found out the young beast had broken some kind of rule and brought a human to the moot.

Ethan got up and padded after Fingal. Dragging his feet, he pretended to check the trees and bushes for more clues to the loremaster's whereabouts. But there'd been no trace of Griffen since the crossroads ten miles back. "We might as well give up," he said. "It's just no use."

Fingal's head swiveled around and he regarded Ethan with sad violet eyes. "No Ethan. A hero does not give up so soon."

"I'm not a hero," Ethan protested.

"You were a hero in Nir. You have been a hero in Cynwyd. You will be a hero here." Fingal sounded so sure of himself that Ethan wondered if the young dragon's power to see the future had returned.

He marched in front of the dragon and addressed the beast in a firm but very formal tone. "Fingal, son of Nemth, son of Alwaid, do you already *know* what's going to happen?" he asked. "And *where* Griffen is?"

Fingal's eyes whirled furiously, then turned several shades of blue. "No. I told you I cannot see what is happening now. And I cannot see the future either. Actually, dragons my age never can see the future, we must — "

Sensing that Fingal was about to launch into a lengthy explanation of dragon development and upbringing, Ethan interrupted, "I would love to hear about what dragons your age can and can't do," he said, "but it's cold and the sun's getting lower. How far are we from the Dragon moot?"

Fingal's eyes filled with pity. "Not far at all." He unsheathed a claw and pointed toward a broad mist-filled valley.

Ethan peered through the fog but, as far as he could tell, no dragons were in sight. "When does the moot start?" he asked.

41

Fingal chuckled. "Moot has been in session for seven golds and seven pearls already."

Ethan paused to digest that. Seven golds and seven pearls meant a week in dragonspeak. "But where are the dragons?"

"Beneath the mist. Dragons, as you know, can be quite invisible unless they want to be seen. Even when they gather in great numbers for a meeting like this." Fingal looked around. Just ahead, a narrow switchback path cut off from the road. It wound past a farmhouse, then seemed to continue toward the valley floor though its end was lost in fog. "I have been thinking of how to bring you to the moot. We will make you look different."

Ethan hurried to keep up as the dragon lumbered into the farm yard. Like the homesteads in Peredur, this one seemed deserted. "You mean, I'll wear some kind of disguise?" he asked.

"You will be an apprentice loremaster," Fingal said as he tapped open the door, and poked his head inside. The rest of him was too big to enter the small cottage, so he backed out and beckoned Ethan in.

Inside, Ethan spied a broad-planked table near the hearth and a couple of chairs. A bed, stripped of its bedding and mattress, hugged one wall, and at its foot was a crudely carved trunk. Hesitantly, Ethan went to the trunk

42

and lifted its lid. He wondered for a moment if borrowing clothes in these circumstances was any different than actually stealing.

To his surprise the trunk was bursting with all sorts of clothing, most of it light and summery. On Fingal's advice, he outfitted himself in a bright striped shirt with billowy sleeves and festive-looking leggings. Over that he put the stout jerkin Olwyn had given him, and on top of everything his thick fur cape.

He darted outside and spun round once so the dragon could inspect him.

"Good," Fingal said with an approving rattle of his scales. "You look exactly like a young loremaster — except — " Fingal paused and blew out a faint plume of smoke. "Except a loremaster's apprentice must have an instrument to play."

Ethan's face fell. "A *musical* instrument?" he moaned. "Oh Fingal, I can't play any instrument. I can't even carry a tune. I knew this was all wrong," he muttered. "I should have never listened to Olwyn. I should have stayed with her and sent Nicholas with you. He can sing up a storm — he's really good at music."

Fingal's eyes whirled green with worry. "We cannot change things now. You are here with me, only a short distance from Dragon moot. You must pretend to be a young apprentice of the lore, or the dragons will not let you join the moot. You might even," he added with a troubled hiss, "be hurt if the elder dragons think you are a spy."

Ethan gulped. "But where will I find an instrument?" Even as he spoke he began to rummage deeper in the trunk until he felt some round wooden objects. Yanking them out, he saw they were attached to a worn leather sack. Ethan stared at them a moment, then started to laugh. "Bagpipes," he exclaimed. "I wonder if I can get them to work."

He bundled the bag under his arm and tried blowing into the shortest pipe. At first nothing but air hissed out. He tried again, and accidentally squeezed the bag. A terrible shrieking sound filled the air. Ethan winced.

Outside the cottage, Fingal thumped his tail against the hard-packed snow with glee. "Wonderful music! A perfect dragon call. You will be the favorite entertainment at the dragon moot. And I will be most honored for bringing you!"

With that the dragon started down the hill, and Ethan followed. They'd only gone a little ways, when Fingal threw back his head and called loudly up toward the sky.

A jangle of answering calls echoed up from below. Fingal turned back to Ethan, one eye spinning purple, the other a happy pure blue. "We are welcome to Dragon moot. We are *very*

44

welcome as I am told there is no loremaster there. The elders are pleased I have brought you."

A few moments later they entered the valley, and Ethan felt himself go weak at the sight that greeted his eyes. The valley was simply wall-to-wall dragons. A steady hum and keening filled the air. Heat from the dragons' bodies and breath had melted the snowpack. The snowmelt rose from the ground in swirls of mist, and the meadow was a sea of mud. The dragons hunkered down on the foggy ground, like massive boulders or odd-shaped stones.

Some instinct made Ethan pull up his hood, and shield his face. "Fingal," he whispered as they squished across the muddy field. "If anyone asks, tell them that where I come from a loremaster's apprentice must hide his face until he has become a journeyman. Then," Ethan went on, beginning to enjoy making up a story, "he must wear a mask."

Fingal peered down his long snout at Ethan and said with great interest. "Is that so? I say I've never heard such a thing, but if that is true for you in Boston, if you really were a loremaster's apprentice then it shall be true for you here. The customs of Boston sound rather fascinating."

Ethan stared after the large beast and tried

45

not to laugh. Apparently, Fingal had taken him at his word. As they moved past the first row of dragons, Ethan murmured with delight. "Ethan Lord, Loremaster of Boston."

Six

Dragon Moot

"Loremaster of Boston," Ethan repeated.

"So that's what you are," thundered a large and very familiar voice. A huge golden claw shot out and snagged Ethan's trailing cape. "I seem to be fresh out of loremasters these days."

Ethan gulped and peered out from under his hood at the scaled foot. Even in the mist it shimmered like a heap of coins. He slowly glanced up the foot, then up the powerful leg and chest and neck until he reached the head. He braced himself to look the dragon straight in his golden eyes. "Angarth?" he blurted out, and craned his neck to look past the huge dragon king in search of the loremaster. He'd found Angarth. Griffen had to be nearby.

Angarth's hold tightened on Ethan's cloak. "How do *you* know my name?" The beast's snort of displeasure was loud, and drew the attention of all the neighboring dragons. Throughout the valley, the pleasant hum and

47

keening stopped. Ethan shook in his boots as the bulky dragons shuffled toward him and Angarth, forming a tight circle around them. Out of the corner of his eye he spotted Fingal inching away, looking rather scared.

"What doesss it matter, Oh Ancient Gilded One? Though his garmentsss are ssstrange, he carriesss the pipes. He can make music," hissed a slight silver and blue dragon wearing a pearl-trimmed crown on its head. It was the first time Ethan had seen a dragon wearing any part of its hoard. Suddenly he was sure the dragon was female. "You, oh mightiessst of the dragonsss, have *sssssaid* you have lost your own loremaster, and now you have found a new one. The fatesss are kind to you, oh king."

"Silence, Lyryn," the dragon king bellowed and blasted the female dragon with a small jet of flame. "The loss of my loremaster is not a small matter. He was *stolen*." Angarth stressed the last word and paused to let his accusation sink in.

"Griffen *stolen!*" Ethan exclaimed in horror, but his comment was lost in the outcry that went up from the dragons gathered nearby.

"Stolen?"

"Dragon-napped!"

"Rubbish," Lyryn scoffed, but soft enough that Angarth didn't seem to hear. "No self-respecting dragon would steal from another drag-

48

on. It takes a thief to know one, that's what I say," she concluded with a thump of her tail that made Ethan jump.

Angarth cleared his throat, and the dragons fell silent. He turned his attention back to Ethan. "So you, with your pipes, have come along at a very convenient time," he said craftily. "But that does not explain how you knew my name — I do not know you."

Ethan bowed as deeply as he could, trying to keep the hood over his face. "Everyone in the Seven Kingdoms, and in the lands beyond, knows of Angarth the Golden."

Ethan's response pleased Angarth. "Said like a true master of the lore."

"I am no master yet," Ethan hurried on to say, his heart thumping double time, "I am a mere apprentice — a *first year* apprentice. Uh — more like first month of first year apprentice."

"Thus the hood, Mighty One." Fingal spoke up from the edge of the crowd. "He is of the Guild of Loremasters of the distant kingdom of Boston, where apprentices are hooded until they become journeymen, when they are masked."

A chorus of interested oohs and ahhs went up from the other dragons.

At the word Boston, Angarth bent low toward Ethan trying to get a better look at him.

"Hmmmm, something familiar there is about you," he muttered. "Boston . . . where have I heard that before?" Still staring at Ethan, he fell into dragonspeak. "*Bosfudystan,* no, no, *Ungarth rymed drysmel thymd,*" he concluded with a puzzled shake of his huge head. "Name. What is your name?"

Ethan spoke before Fingal had a chance. "Uh — names — yes, about names. Well, in my guild I can't have a name until I'm a full loremaster. I have to — uh — prove myself first. Do something sort of — uh — important," he finished lamely.

"Like me," Fingal said sounding very impressed. He had worked his way up closer to Ethan. "You must tell me more about this guild when you get the chance," he said cheerily. "You seem to have some of the same rules for young loremasters-to-be that we have for young dragons who have not yet glimpsed the heart of fire."

Ethan cringed. "Quiet, Fingal. Something's happened to Griffen and we've got to find out *what.* It sounds like he's in big trouble."

Meanwhile, Angarth rocked back and forth on his haunches muttering to himself. Finally he reared up and boomed a pronouncement. "I will call you, Apprentice. You will replace my own Loremaster, Griffen of Nir, until the thief who has stolen him, returns him."

Ethan nodded weakly.

The dragon king extended one great claw and tapped a low tree stump. "Stand here and spell us a tale with music," he commanded Ethan. "This moot is in need of entertaining before the real discussion begins."

Ethan froze.

Angarth's golden scales darkened slightly. "Apprentice, do you not hear me? Begin."

"Here goes nothing," Ethan mumbled as he went over to the stump. Ethan closed his fingers around the bagpipes and tried to take a deep breath. Closing his eyes, he blew as hard as he could into the pipe and squeezed the leather bag.

A horrible squeak filled the valley, nearly deafening Ethan but obviously pleasing the dragons. Roars and grunts of approval went up from the crowd. Ethan randomly blew on first one pipe then another, and played several awful notes. He stopped, but the dragons were listening politely, and so he took another deep breath and played on.

The dragons let him play for what seemed like several hours. At last Angarth raised one golden claw, and Ethan gratefully stopped. "Not bad for an apprentice," the dragon king commented. "Though not nearly as soothing as Griffen's music. Now," he turned to glare at Lyryn. "The moot will come to order and attend to the real business of the day: my stolen Lore-master."

"It takes a thief to know one!" Lyryn said for the second time.

Angarth growled, then looked down at Ethan. "This is dragon talk. You, as an apprentice, cannot be privy to it. Griffen's guild would not let you."

"But attending moots is part of my training with the Guild of Boston," Ethan said, desperate to get any clues as to Griffen's whereabouts.

"We are not in Boston here," said Angarth, his hackles rising.

"Uh — right," Ethan agreed quickly, taking a few steps backward. "But where do I go?"

"Go with that young creature who brought you. At the end of the moot you will come with me. I need company."

Ethan let out a disappointed sigh, but had no choice but to obey. He climbed on Fingal's outstretched wing, and then onto his back. Moments later Fingal deposited him on a cliff overlooking the valley. He brushed some twigs together with his wings, and blew on them to start a fire.

"You will be warm here, until either Angarth or I return for you."

"But where are you going?" Ethan cried.

"To the moot, I may be young but I get a vote too."

"What are you voting about?" Ethan tried again to get information.

"I do not know," responded Fingal honestly. "As I told you, the transmissions are unclear. I will soon learn though. Obviously whatever happened to Griffen has caused a rift between the dragons, or there would be no moot, and no vote."

With that Fingal flew off, leaving Ethan by the small fire. Ethan sat cross-legged on the snowy ground. The sun was just going down over the mountains to the west. *One more day that Griffen's missing,* Ethan thought to himself. He hugged his knees to his chest, feeling cold and alone.

Seven

The Dragon Queen

"Leave it to Ethan," Nicholas grumbled as he and Olwyn toiled up the steep slope, "to run off and hang out with dragons and leave us with the dirty work."

They had been scaling the mountain all day. The switchback road had dwindled to a narrow footpath, then about an hour ago, on the edge of a high rocky meadow, it gave out entirely. The north wind was fierce and constant. It swept down from the cloud wreathed summit, clearing the snow from that side of the mountain.

Now it was late afternoon and the shadows were deepening. "I just bet you Ethan's nice and warm right now," Nicholas concluded through chattering teeth.

Olwyn wasn't listening. She climbed slowly and carefully a few feet above Nicholas, picking her way through the jagged rocks and boulders. They were headed toward a high plateau above the clouds that they had spotted from the meadow.

"Nicholas, look up there, to your right," Olwyn yelled back over her shoulder. "Griffen's left another clue."

Eagerly, Nicholas worked his way toward the cliff face. A scrubby oak grew straight out of the rock, it's short limbs twisted from the wind. Snagged on a branch was a scrap of brightly embroidered linen, much like the one Nicholas had spotted earlier in the meadow. "Another bit of your father's shirt sleeve." Nicholas grinned at Olwyn. "We haven't lost the trail."

"Not yet," Olwyn warned, pointing west. The pale winter sun hovered low in the sky. "We'd better cover as much ground as we can before dark." She craned her neck and looked up. In the last hour they had traveled farther than she thought. The cloud that circled the high reaches of the mountain was only a few yards away. It blocked the view of the plateau where they planned to pitch camp.

A few moments later they plunged into the swirling mists. "I've never walked inside a cloud before," Nicholas said. "And I can't say I've missed much." He felt as if he was walking through an icy rain. The cold stung his cheeks and blurred his vision. The wind and the sheer effort of the climb made it impossible to speak.

Then suddenly, just when Nicholas was sure his legs would give out under him, the ground leveled off. A few more steps and he walked into a blaze of bright sunlight.

The plateau where they stood, was not as large as it seemed from below. Actually, it wasn't a plateau at all: just a deep ledge cut into the side of the mountain, and sheltered from the winter gales by the cliff that lead to the summit itself.

"And look," Olwyn cried as she spotted another scrap of cloth flapping in the breeze. "My father's come this way too. For a minute back there in the fog I was sure we'd lost him."

All at once the hopeful expression vanished from Olwyn's face. The color drained from her cheeks.

"What's wrong?" Nicholas asked.

Olwyn turned around to face him, her blue-grey eyes troubled. "I sense a secret here — " She stopped and very slowly scanned the ground before them. "There's something ancient nearby, something from before — " Olwyn's sentence ended with a sharp intake of breath. "Oh no," she moaned. Then forgetting their decision to be cautious and keep near cover, Olwyn bolted across the clearing toward a lone dwarfed pine. She dropped to her knees in the snow.

"What happened?" Nicholas asked, running

up. Then he saw a heap of rags half covered with snow.

Carefully Olwyn brushed the snow off the rags. "My father," she said brokenly. "These are his clothes." Tenderly, she gathered up the tattered garments. "Something must have attacked him. He — if he was wearing these — he couldn't have survived."

Nicholas stared dumbly at the remnants of the loremaster's clothing. Looking closely, he recognized Griffen's thick leather jerkin, his black hooded cape and a scrap of linen from his shirt. Suddenly, a vision of Griffen floated into his head. Nicholas fought back tears from his own eyes. Why would anyone hurt such a wise and gentle man? Nicholas knelt down next to Olwyn and fingered Griffen's torn fur cape. But as he touched it he realized what was wrong.

"Olwyn," he began, "there's no blood on these clothes, and — " But before he could say more, a dark shadow fell across them. He glanced up just as a flurry of rocks crashed down from the peak above. The small avalanche miraculously ended at his feet.

"Tressssssspassssers!" hissed a voice from the sky.

Nicholas's head snapped up and he threw out his arms to shield Olwyn. An enormous shadow wheeled across the sun, blotting out the last of its light.

"Humansssss! In my lair!"

A great flap of wings. The rattle of a thousand scales. The horrible scratchy sound of talons scraping against bare rock. Then the creature lit down, only a yard from Nicholas.

Nicholas grabbed Olwyn's arm, and forced her behind him against the wall of the cliff. Only then did he dare to look up at the creature.

It was a dragon, all right, but different from any dragon Nicholas had ever seen. Its pearly-white scales shimmered like a rainbow in the sunset. Though far more slender and graceful, it was taller than Angarth, and definitely younger. Nicholas stared a moment, fascinated by the strand of pearls dangling from its neck and the jewels that encrusted its scales. It looked like the dragon was wearing its hoard.

He made the mistake of looking directly into the dragon's eyes — and realized he was powerless to look away. The huge rainbow-colored eyes blazed with fury — and pain. *This is it,* Nicholas thought. *It's going to kill us now.*

The dragon's mammoth jaws opened as it let out an ear-splitting screech. Terrified, Nicholas watched it rear up on its hind legs and belch out a ribbon of fire. Then it roared and the earth shook. Boulders cascaded from the ledge above their heads. Nicholas shielded his face with his arms. But the rocks landed at his feet in a half circle. When the rockslide stopped, he and Olwyn were penned inside a low rock wall.

Olwyn stepped forward, her white face streaked with tears, but her eyes dark with anger. "The Dragon Queen," she gasped. "You murdered my father!" Then before Nicholas could stop her, Olwyn leaped over the wall and flung herself at the huge beast, pounding the dragon's massive haunches with her fists. At last, she collapsed weeping on the ground.

Berwyn was clearly taken aback. She was still rearing on her back legs, ready to attack Olwyn. But with great grace she backed toward the entrance to a dark cave. She settled her front paws on the ground, several feet shy of the sobbing girl.

"Sssso humans really do cry," she muttered, and shook her head in dismay. "How can I kill ssssomething with feelingsss worthy of a dragon?"

Nicholas crept over to Olwyn to pull her away from the dragon. Berwyn gave herself a shake and the pearls around her neck clicked against the delicate scales of her underside. "And you?" she demanded of Nicholas. "What are you doing here?"

Nicholas's knees felt like noodles. "I'm here to help Olwyn find her father. What have you done with him?"

"Stop it, Nicholas," Olwyn ordered through

her tears. She looked up and wiped her face with the sleeve of her jerkin. "Nothing we say or do can bring him back now."

Berwyn growled from deep in her chest, "No one hasss been killed — not yet."

Olwyn gasped. "My father — he's alive?"

"Inssside the cave."

"Griffen!" Olwyn shouted at the top of her lungs. "Father! Answer me."

All Olwyn heard was the echo of her own words. Olwyn snapped her head around and glared at Berwyn. "You *say* he's alive, but I don't believe you. I won't believe you until I see him."

Berwyn paused and buffed a long talon against the soft scales of her belly. "Then look," she said craftily, and eased her bulk away from the front of the cave.

Olwyn raced past her, but Nicholas held back. Berwyn was a dragon. She shouldn't be able to lie, but he was sure he couldn't trust her. What if Griffen weren't really there? What if she tried to trap them inside the cave? He narrowed his eyes and looked up again at Berwyn. She was sitting back on her haunches looking very smug. Suddenly it occurred to him that female dragons might play by a different set of rules.

"Nicholas, come quickly! He's here." Olwyn's voice was full of pain. "But something's wrong. He can't talk to me. He can't even move his hands."

Nicholas stopped just long enough to give Berwyn a dirty look. Then he plunged into the cave.

Meanwhile on the cliff overlooking the Valley of the Lost Dragon, Ethan had drifted into a restless sleep. He tossed and turned through nightmares of dark, shadowy dragons, and finally awoke with a jolt. Embers of Fingal's fire still smoldered. All at once the memory flooded back to him. He was on a high mountain ledge far above the valley, waiting for Fingal.

Ethan felt another jolt. The entire mountain was shaking! Earthquake, was his first thought. Then he realized the shaking had a definite thump, thump-de-thump sort of rhythm. He pulled his glasses out of his pocket, put them on and got to his feet. The darkness was thick and foggy. Neither the moon nor the stars were out. But a rainbow mist spiraled upward from where the Dragon moot was still in session.

He felt his way along the cliff wondering if there were some way down. If only he had a flashlight. Ethan thought a minute then looked over at the smoldering remains of his fire and got an idea. He rooted around on the ground until he found a thick, dried branch, which he held to the embers. In moments he had a real torch.

Ethan only half-believed he'd find a way down into the valley. So he was startled when the light flickered on what looked like a very deep and high step, leading down along one side of the ledge. "Stairs?" He held the torch up high, and sure enough, he spied a second step, and part of a third. Whatever was beyond the third step lay in shadows.

"Here goes nothing," Ethan said aloud. Then, very slowly and carefully, he began to climb down the steep, snow-covered steps.

Half-an-hour later, Ethan reached the bottom. He realized he was not far from where he and Fingal had first entered the moot. Thick brush and thickets of bare trees blocked his view, though from where he stood the thumping sound was almost deafening. He crept closer and pushed aside the last few branches. The sight that met his eyes was so astounding, he forgot for a moment to crouch low and keep out of sight.

Hundreds of dragons were lined up in two long rows, each row stretching farther than Ethan could see. But up close he recognized Angarth, and opposite him the female dragon, Lyryn. Suddenly, Ethan realized they were dancing, and the keening sound that filled the air, was their song. They swayed back and forth and slapped their wings together behind them, and arched and swung their long necks around in slow, dignified circles. Ethan knelt down on the snow, and watched spellbound from his hiding place. The dance and song seemed to go on forever, then suddenly the keening stopped, and everyone grew still.

Ethan sat up straight and tried to listen to the dragon's talk. Lyryn's snakelike voice carried clearly across the frosty night air.

"Dragonnsssssss never lie," she began. "To lie issss to lossse the rightsss of dragonhood and to be plunged into the darknessss at the depthss of the earth forever."

"Whom, Lyryn, do you accuse of lying?" Angarth's answer boomed across the clearing.

"You, oh mightiesssst of the mighty dragonssss. You who claim to be above such thingsss."

Ethan was surprised to hear a chorus of dragons hissing their agreement with Lyryn. Then for the first time he noticed that one long line of dragons looked very different from the other. Like Lyryrn, jewels glittered on their scales. "Girl dragons," he whispered and wondered if the enraged Queen Berwyn was there.

Angarth growled from deep in his throat, and the ground shook. Lyryn didn't look impressed.

"What am I lying about?"

64

Silently Ethan cheered Angarth for sounding so dignified.

"Your preciousss loremaster. You say Berwyn sssstole him. But Berwyn issss no thief. We the motherssss are here to prove that. We know exactly how you injured Berwyn. We sssseek the right of the lair to prove it."

"The right of the lair!" Several male dragons exclaimed in horror. "The right of *Angarth's lair*. Never!"

"Never," Angarth echoed. "Never shall that thief or any of the mothers invade my lair. I have never stolen to nourish my hoard. Not in the thousands of years of my life — not once!"

Ethan cringed as the line of male dragons took a threatening step forward, toward the smaller bejeweled "mothers."

"You dare threaten me at a moot?" Lyryn challenged Angarth, her voice haughty and proud. "You dare to break centuriesss of tradition? Thissss is a place of peace. We shall not break the peace — *here*. But if it isss war you want, the motherssss will do anything to protect the right of their hatchlings. To protect their — "

"Enough," boomed Angarth. He slapped his tail hard against the packed snow. "I have not threatened you." He looked down the line of male dragons, and let out a dangerous growl. "And whoever breaks the peace of this moot

65

will be put to death."

Lyryn actually bowed her head. "It isss good then, to see you honor some principlesss. But I have called the moot at Berwyn's request. Thisss matter means life and death to all of usss, male and female dragons alike. Thus, I want a vote. Do we seek a battle ground to sssettle this issue once and for all? The mothers against the others. Or will we have the right of Angarth's lair?"

"Why isn't Berwyn here?" Angarth voiced the very question on Ethan's mind.

"Because she mussssst find what has been ssstolen, before it is too late." Lyryn paused then added, "And because she fears your spiesss will try to capture Griffen."

"You admit she has stolen Griffen!" Angarth's bellow knocked Ethan off his feet.

Lyryn arched her graceful neck and looked down her snout at the dragon king. "She hasss *borrowed* your precious loremaster. He is hossstage until you return what is rightfully hers."

"Griffen has nothing to do with this matter!" the dragon king roared. "You must return him — unharmed. He is not just valuable to me. He is precious to the lore of the whole Seven Kingdoms. The lore predicts that only Griffen can bring Nir its lost king."

Lyryn swung her head back and forth.

"Trussst ussss. He will not be hurt — not permanently," she added, and Ethan's blood ran cold. Why couldn't Angarth force her to lead him to Griffen?

"If you do not return what is Berwyn's," Lyryn went on, "she will not return what is yoursss."

Ethan had heard enough. Wearily, he began to make his way back toward the steps to the ledge. Fingal would look for him there in the morning, so he'd better be there. But in the meantime, his mind was whirling with questions: What was the Right of Angarth's Lair. And would Angarth really steal something?

"Here's what I know," he reasoned aloud. "Angarth has something that belongs to Berwyn, and he won't give it back. And Berwyn's willing to start a dragon war over it — and poor Griffen is caught in the middle."

Eight

The Curse

Berwyn's cave wasn't dark. Soft luminous light seeped through the lichen-coated walls. In one corner a low fire burned, and huddled with her back toward it was Olwyn. Beside her, propped against the wall, like a sack of flour, was her father, Griffen, Loremaster of Nir.

"Griffen!" Nicholas scrambled over to the older man's side.

Griffen looked up with wide bright eyes, and smiled at Nicholas. He looked very frail and very foolish. His long, white beard was full of burrs, and he wore only a pair of torn breeches and a tattered green cloak. Nicholas ripped off his own fur cape and draped it over the loremaster's shoulders.

"What's wrong with him?" Olwyn asked. "He smiles, he looks at me, but he doesn't talk — "

Nicholas shook his head. "I don't know." He thought a moment. "Can you hear me?" he asked The Loremaster.

Griffen nodded vigorously.

Olwyn sat up straighter and took both her father's hands in hers. "Father, are you all right — have you eaten?" Griffen nodded again and gestured toward a pile of fruit in the corner.

"So Berwyn really is keeping you alive." Olwyn breathed a sigh of relief. Then she spotted Griffen's lute — or what was left of it. The shards of polished inlaid wood lay in a heap against the wall. "Your lute!" she cried.

Nicholas saw the ruined instrument, and bounded back out the cave entrance. "What have you done to him?" he demanded of the dragon queen. "Why did you break his lute? You might as well have killed him!"

Berwyn, who was preening her scales, gave Nicholas a lazy, disinterested look. But when she answered she chose her words carefully, and Nicholas knew then that female dragons had at least one thing in common with the males: They had to tell the truth.

"I have cursssed him," she stated. "He made the misstake of being in the wrong place at the wrong time. Besssides, Angarth valuesss him. Whatever Angarth valuessss, I will dessstroy. I have taken away his voice, his sssstories — I do not know what Angarth sees in those stories; they bore me." Berwyn yawned. Nicholas staggered at the sight of hundreds of daggerlike teeth. "And ," she went on, "his arms are now uselessss. He will never play an inssstrument again."

"But that's like killing him," Nicholas said angrily. "Without his music, a loremaster just withers away. And so — " Nicholas said suddenly inspired, "So does the lore of the Seven Kingdoms. So does *your* story, Berwyn."

Nicholas's words produced the right effect. "Berwyn," the dragon queen mused softly, "Daughter of Laird, Daughter of Calyx, Daughter of Dryffyd, Daughter of Rhyrron — " She winced as if in pain. "Even my story will die out. That then is the real curse of Peredur. All the tales will die — we will all disappear. Angarth will have even that," she murmured.

"What has Angarth done to you?" Nicholas asked.

The pale dragon whirled on him. "How dare you ask that? You are his sssssspies, aren't you? You were sent here to find out the truth — about that idiot loremaster. Yessss," she spat, and her breath was so hot the scrub oaks fringing the cave went up in smoke. "I ssssstole that worthless bag of bones from Angarth, and I would do it again. Angarth is a thief — he has ssssstolen from me what I value most in the world. Am I, Berwyn, Queen of all the Dragons, Mother of Cyrryn, Krystol, and Pyrdarth, to sit back and have no revenge?"

"Angarth a thief?" Nicholas couldn't believe it.

"What has he stolen?" Olwyn spoke up from the entrance of the cave. Her father was by her side, a pale, thin version of his formerly plump self.

At least he can walk, Nicholas thought. Immediately, he began scanning the clearing for an escape route.

Berwyn apparently read his mind. "There is no escape — "

"How did you — "

"I know everything," Berwyn said proudly.

"But Fingal said the channels that link the minds of dragons with each other and with people are blocked."

"Who do you think blocked them?" Berwyn snapped.

"Never mind that," Olwyn snapped back. "You haven't answered my question. What has Angarth stolen? And what in the world does my father have to do with it?" Seeing that she was getting no answer from the dragon, Olwyn helped Griffen over to a large flat stone, and gently eased him down.

"Well, girl child," said the dragon queen, who was now watching her with interest. "I see you have feelings worthy of a dragon. You care for your father. He cares for you. I imagine you will ssssomeday care for your own child."

"Perhaps," Olwyn answered carefully. "If I live through this — if you will tell me your story. I may be able to help you."

"Help *me*?" Berwyn bristled.

"I am a loremaster too," Olwyn said quickly. "Or will be soon. If there's trouble between you and Angarth, it is part of my work — and my father's — to set it right."

For a long moment the dragon queen was silent, and when she answered her voice was filled with grief. "Angarth has stolen the queen egg of my clutch. He has stolen my future from me!"

"I don't believe you," Olwyn said quietly.

Berwyn's eyes whirled dangerously. "I do not care what you believe." she hissed. "Child of man, you know nothing of dragons. Angarth has stolen."

"When?" Olwyn asked at the same time Nicholas asked, "Why?"

Berwyn brushed off Olwyn's question with a flick of her tail. "I do not know when." She hissed and steam wreathed up into the sky, clouding the moon. "But the time of hatching is near. If I do not get my egg back, my dragonling will die. Then," she raised her voice and began to keen, her wail rising into the wind, "Angarth will die too."

"So it's not just a jewel that's been stolen!"

Olwyn exclaimed, and looked with pity on the grief-stricken queen. "It's her child!"

"But why would Angarth steal an egg?" Nicholas asked.

"Greed. There issssss nothing more beautiful in a Mother's hoard than her Queen egg. Nothing," Berwyn replied. "And nothing more precious."

Olwyn shook her head. "I understand your pain, Berwyn. I felt it long before I met you. I felt somehow I could help you, that the fates had entangled our lives together."

"You and I, entangled by the fatesss," Berwyn scoffed.

"Careful Berwyn," Olwyn said, a note of command in her voice. "You must not curse the Loremasters of the Seven Kingdoms. We have our powers too. Our stories sometimes come true."

Nicholas braced himself, fearful that Berwyn would choose to strike Olwyn dumb like her father.

Instead Berwyn seemed to back down. "I will lisssten then. How can you ssssteal my egg back from Angarth?"

"I didn't promise that," Olwyn said quickly, then chose her next words with great care. "I can help you find your egg. I can see if Angarth has it. But I don't believe he is a thief because dragons don't steal."

Nicholas shook his head. "That's not true, Olwyn. Berwyn has stolen Griffen from Angarth."

"Ssssshrewd you are!" Berwyn growled. "But I have not stolen him — I will return him — in exchange for what is rightfully mine."

Nicholas let out an exasperated cry. "But what if Angarth doesn't have your egg?"

"But he doesssss, Nicholas of Boston. He doesssss."

"No Berwyn. He *might* have your egg — unless of course you have proof." Olwyn said firmly.

"Proof?" Berwyn seemed startled at the word. "What proof do I need? Who else is powerful enough to invade my hoard — to cast a spell deep enough to fool me?"

"I don't know," Olwyn admitted. "But I promise you, if you let us go to Angarth we'll find out. Nicholas and his brother have done Angarth the great favor of returning the pearl Peacemaker to him — "

"You are the hero of the Peacemaker tale?" Berwyn eyed Nicholas skeptically.

Nicholas bowed modestly. "One of them. Griffen, Olwyn and my brother helped, too."

"So Angarth is indebted to you," Berwyn frowned at Nicholas.

Olwyn looked at her father who was shaking his head back and forth.

74

Berwyn's voice turned smooth as silk. "Then Angarth will do — *must* do — everything to help you. Ssssurely, he will not want to see you harmed — "

Olwyn's hand flew to her mouth. "Don't Berwyn. Don't enspell him too."

Berwyn turned a kindly rainbow eye on the girl. "Enssspell him?" She shrugged and her jeweled scales sparkled in the moonlight. "I would not bother. I will only keep him here. As — a pledge that you will return with the egg."

"But you already have my father," Olwyn wailed.

"I will keep your father if the egg is not returned. But Nicholas — he is disssposable. As you said, I cannot really harm a loremassster."

Nicholas gaped at the dragon queen. "You — you'll kill me?"

"Now, now. I expected more courage from a hero of the Kingdom of Bossston." Berwyn looked down her snout at Nicholas scornfully. "I will not kill you if Angarth returnsss my egg. If he doesn't — " Her eyes locked on Nicholas and the blood in his veins seemed to turn to ice.

Turning back to Olwyn, Berwyn said. "We leave for Angarth's lair at firssst light. All of you will spend the night in the cave." Her eyes flashed a warning. "And don't wassste time trying to escape. There is no way to leave my lair — sssssafely." Her hiss slithered into a grim sort of laugh. "Girl child, I will fly you close to Angarth's Peak, high in the mountains of Nir. I cannot approach the lair itself, as he has cast a ssspell to keep me out. But you are not a dragon. He does not fear any creature that climbs on two legs to such heightsss."

With that, Berwyn herded her three captives back into the cave. Then she settled her bulk in front of it, and sealed their prison for the night.

Nine

Maps and Masks

True to her word, Berwyn roused Olwyn at first light and they started out — but not before Berwyn plugged the entrance to the cave with a small avalanche of ice and rocks. "You'll be safe in there," the Dragon Queen called to Griffen and Nicholas, "until I return." Then, with a whooosh of her wings, she took off.

Several hours later, Nicholas took his umpteenth walk to the back of the cave. A river of jewels and gold and assorted treasure, tumbled out of a passage to the right. Berwyn's hoard was impressive, even by dragon standards.

"Why would Angarth steal an egg?" he asked Griffen, even though he knew the Loremaster couldn't answer. "He could have stolen half of this stuff." Nicholas bent down, picked up a gold crown, and set the object on his head. He peered into a shiny silver platter, just to see how he looked. The circlet of gold was studded with rubies and diamonds and fit his head perfectly.

"King Nicholas," he murmured, grinning at his reflection.

But it wasn't long before even King Nicholas was restless and bored and itched to find a way to escape. "Oh, Griffen," he said as he threw the crown back on the pile and flopped down next to the fire. "Something about this place is so familiar. I feel like I've seen it before — the cave, the mountains outside." He looked at the loremaster. "Do you know what I mean?"

Griffen nodded so forcefully, Nicholas sat right up again.

"Do *you* know something about this place — some way to escape?"

Griffen heaved a deep breath. He eased himself into a more comfortable position. Then carefully, he shook his head "yes."

Nicholas knelt up and leaned forward. "You're trying to tell me something — something about this cave. There *is* a way out."

Griffen nodded vigorously.

"So I have to guess where this back door might be." Nicholas got up with a sigh and began searching the cave again. With exactly as much luck as he'd had before.

Not quite ready to give up, Nicholas shot some more questions at the loremaster. Lots of nodding went on, but still Nicholas couldn't fathom what Griffen was trying to tell him. Finally he said, "If only you could use your hands, you could make me a map."

At the word map, Griffen nodded vigorously.

"You mean there's a map here somewhere?" Nicholas held his breath waiting for Griffen's answer.

The loremaster shook his head and bit his lip hard.

"But I don't have a map to the Seven Kingdoms — " Nicholas's voice trailed off. He jumped up and looked down at the loremaster. "That's what you've been trying to tell me. I *have seen* a map that can show us the way out."

Griffen nodded carefully.

"You're right — there were maps I saw in Breton's study." Nicholas tried to piece together the facts aloud. "There was even one of Peredur." He dropped down to the floor again and closed his eyes, trying to remember exactly what he had seen when he had been an apprentice to Nir's most evil sorcerer.

All at once Nicholas could picture the map that had been on Breton's wall. He had spent a lot of time looking at it because it was filled with wonderful drawings of dragons and mountains and flying castles. Up in the section that showed the Northern Reaches there'd been a drawing of a cave, and from the cave there was a tunnel. It ended in a splotch of ink then seemed to rise again out of the earth and lead to someplace back in the Kingdom of Nir.

"By the Pearl," Nicholas exclaimed, springing to his feet. "There's a tunnel from here, and it goes to Angarth's lair!"

Griffen beamed.

"So what are we waiting for?" Nicholas said, pulling the loremaster to his feet. "I know you're not feeling very strong," he went on, realizing a journey underground might be too much for the older man. "But I'm afraid to leave you here. If Berwyn returns and finds me gone and you — "

Griffen closed his eyes then opened them, and took a few faltering steps toward the back of the cave.

"You don't know the way either, do you, Griffen?" Suddenly the fact Griffen hadn't tried to escape made sense. "You just knew the lore."

Griffen confirmed this with a nod.

"So it's up to me — but," Nicholas stopped and gulped. "But this way out is not as simple as it looks, is it?"

Griffen shook his head.

"I should have realized. Berwyn wouldn't leave the tunnel unguarded — especially if it leads to her precious hoard." Nicholas shrugged, wondering whether to risk the tunnel or the dragon queen's return. "Do you still want to try it?" he asked the loremaster.

Griffen nodded a definite yes.

The map in Nicholas's mind pointed to a small tunnel opposite the one bursting with Berwyn's hoard. Slowly, he felt his way along the wall. Here at the back of the cave, the lichen on the walls was sparse and gave out little light. To his right and a little ways above his head there seemed to be a hint of a warm breeze. A moment later he found a round opening in the wall. He had to jump a little to reach it, and dangled a moment by his fingers before hoisting himself over its edge. Then, he leaned out, and reached down to grab Griffen's wrists to haul him up.

Griffen scrambled as best he could using his feet, and at last lay panting beside Nicholas on the tunnel floor. "Well, we've managed step one," Nicholas declared with forced cheerfulness.

The roof of the tunnel was so low that both the boy and the loremaster had to stoop as they walked. After a few minutes, Nicholas's whole body was aching. He groped along the tunnel wall with one hand and held Griffen's arm with the other.

The tunnel continued steadily downward, and soon the ceiling was high enough for them to stand upright.

Griffen suddenly made an effort to speak. "Griffen," Nicholas exclaimed, "is Berwyn's power weaker down here?"

Griffen answered with a shrug, then a nod, then a shake of his head.

"It's something else, isn't it?"

Griffen hesitated but nodded.

"But you don't know what."

Griffen didn't answer that.

Nicholas sighed deeply. It was too late to turn back now. He grabbed Griffen's hand and continued their trek deep into the heart of the mountains.

On a high cliff overlooking the Valley of the Lost Dragon, a cold blast of wind awakened Ethan. He huddled there, shivering and very discouraged. It was nearly noon, and Fingal hadn't come for him. Even worse, there was a war brewing that he couldn't stop. He knew where Griffen was, but had no way of finding Berwyn. Ethan was just beginning to wonder if he had been abandoned when Angarth sailed into view.

The king dragon's golden scales glinted in the sun as he indulged in a fancy loop-the-loop before folding back his wings into a vee and plummeting toward Ethan. The enormous beast landed on the ledge with the gracefulness of a sparrow.

"It sure took you long enough," Ethan said, forgetting he was supposed to be a lowly apprentice. "How long do moots last anyway?"

82

Angarth looked down at the boy. The wind gusted around the cliff face and pushed Ethan's hood down father over his eyes. Angarth lowered his head trying to peer beneath it.

Ethan put his hand up to shield his face. "You must not see my face. It is the rule of my guild. Back in Boston, first year apprentices must be heard and not seen. I am not worthy to be seen by someone as magnificent as you," he added with a burst of inspiration.

Angarth snorted some smoke rings and sighed. "I feel I know you from somewhere." He paused so long, Ethan gulped. Then the dragon went on, sounding a little befuddled. "But I have met so many people over the centuries." With that he motioned for Ethan to hop on his back. "I will take you to my lair. There you will entertain me until the messengers from the moot arrive with the results of the vote."

Ethan climbed on Angarth's back and held on tight as Angarth took off, wheeling high into the blue afternoon sky. Being a powerful, very large dragon, he flew higher and more swiftly than Fingal. Within moments of takeoff he soared into a bank of puffy clouds.

Ethan shut his eyes. To take his mind off the dizzying flight he tried to remember every knock-knock joke he'd ever heard. By the time Angarth reached the border between Peredur and Nir, Ethan had come up with six jokes and told them to Angarth. Dragons, he soon learned, preferred the bagpipes to knock-knock jokes.

Ethan was debating trying to play the bag-pipes mid-flight when the familiar outline of Angarth's mountain appeared. He'd climbed it three months ago with Griffen on their quest for the Pearl. "We're almost there!" he cried with relief.

"How do you know that?" Angarth inquired.

Ethan winced. He'd forgotten he was sup-posed to be a stranger who'd never been to Nir. But before he could come up with a rea-sonable alibi, Angarth let out a bloodcurdling roar.

"Someone has invaded my lair!" the dragon bellowed. Then he nose dived toward the fright-fully narrow perch in front of his cave.

Ethan grasped one of the sharp spines on Angarth's neck and held on for dear life, but Angarth shook the boy off his back as if he were a flea. "The thief — " the beast reared up with rage. "The thief is still here!"

With that he plunged into the cave. Ethan heard the sound of crashing metal and falling objects. Then finally a terrible scream. It was a girl's voice — one that Ethan would recognize anywhere.

"Olwyn!" cried Ethan, and he bolted into the cave to save her.

"Angarth, stop!" Ethan cried, ripping off his cloak. "Stop right now. We're here to help you!"

The dragon king spun around. He clutched Olwyn in his talon. Hot plumes of steam and smoke and fire bellowed out of his mouth. Even if he didn't squash Olwyn to death, she was certainly in danger of being burned.

"Angarth, I'm your friend. So is Olwyn." Ethan planted himself directly in front of the furious beast. "You know me. I'm Ethan Lord, from Boston. The boy who helped you get Peacemaker back. And that's Olwyn, Griffen's daughter. Please don't hurt her."

The great beast blinked and looked Ethan up and down. A spark of recognition flashed in his huge golden eyes. For a moment he almost seemed to smile, then his eyes began to whirl until they were red with anger. "I did know you — and called you a friend. But now you tell me lies. Why have you told me you're an apprentice loremaster?"

Angarth sounded so disappointed that Ethan blushed and fought a moment to find his voice. He knew that to win back Angarth's trust he'd have to tell the whole truth — no matter what the cost. "Without my disguise as a loremaster, no one would have let me into the moot," he began. Then Ethan went on to tell the story of Griffen's mysterious disappearance, Olwyn's

85

search and the rampages of the Dragon Queen.

"But Olwyn's not stealing from your hoard," Ethan finished. Then he turned to Olwyn. "Tell him you're not. Tell him you're here to help him."

Angarth peered intently at the girl he held in his talon. She closed her eyes to avoid his glance. "I can't. I can't tell him that." She took a very deep breath. "I'm here, because I believe you really do have Berwyn's egg."

The mention of Berwyn and her egg made Angarth roar with rage. "I have no egg. Why would I want an egg?" He turned angrily on Ethan. "You tell me this girl is a friend but — "

"I *am* a friend," Olwyn interrupted, still squirming in Angarth's grasp. "Put me down. I'm Griffen's daughter. You know me." Olwyn pushed back her hair and lifted her face toward the dragon's.

The dragon had only seen her once before, the night the evil sorcerer was defeated in Nir. Angarth studied her then nodded slowly in recognition. But he didn't loosen his hold.

"And I didn't call you a thief, you know," Olwyn went on boldly. "Berwyn did. She's angry and frightened. Her egg is missing and — "

"And I did not steal it," Angarth insisted.

"Please," Ethan begged. "Set Olwyn free. I know she won't hurt you. Besides, I want to know exactly how she got here, and where I can find Nicholas."

"Berwyn's got him," Olwyn said. "She's barricaded him in her lair with Griffen. She's cast a spell so my father can't speak, and she's broken his lute. If I don't find Berwyn's egg, she'll keep Griffen forever — and that will mean the end of all lore in the Seven Kingdoms." Olwyn looked down and sadly added, "And Nicholas will be killed. She's sworn to it."

Ten

Eggnapped

The tunnel seemed endless. It descended steadily downward and widened with every turn. A reddish glow seeped through the walls. It's hotter than the Mojave Desert, thought Nicholas. He wanted to believe he and Griffen would actually come up on the other side of the mountain range, in Nir, thousands of feet in the air where it would be cool again, and he could breathe.

Ahead the road dipped sharply, and then vanished around a curve. Nicholas stopped and took a deep breath. He turned toward Griffen and asked, "Do we just go on?"

Griffen nodded slowly.

"Are we almost at the bottom?"

Griffen nodded.

"Well, let's hope it doesn't get much hotter than this," Nicholas said.

A sloshing, roaring noise like a vast waterfall came up from below. "Hot springs," Nicholas guessed. And indeed, as they turned the corner they saw a lava lake that seemed to stretch for miles. Near the smoldering shore the lava flowed slowly, but toward the center of the lake it moved with the force of a mighty river, then tumbled down into unseen depths below.

Then Nicholas heard another sound — a low moaning. It sounded as if something very large was in terrible pain.

Nicholas braced himself against the ridged wall. "Something's down here," he said to Griffen. He turned and the loremaster's eyes were wide and full of pity.

"You knew that didn't you?"

Griffen nodded.

"Will it hurt us?"

Griffen shrugged, shook his head no, then yes.

Nicholas never had a chance to figure this out. As he stared at the lava lake he realized that the strange shape along its shore was a creature the likes of which he had never before seen. It looked part snake and part dragon. It was red and slimy and wrinkled. Coils of it were draped above the lakeshore, dangling from the black pumice cliffs.

The creature's head was only yards away from Nicholas's feet. Nicholas stiffened, waiting for the snakelike creature to uncoil and pounce.

Griffen grunted. Nicholas spun around. It was the first sound the loremaster had made, and he was pale from the effort of it. But he gestured with his head and Nicholas followed his gaze.

The creature lifted his head with great effort, its pale eyes focused on Nicholas. Suddenly Nicholas got the impression that the lava beast was older than the earth itself, far older than the dragons, or any other creatures that lived this side of time.

The beast glared at Nicholas and moved his head slowly up and down, letting out a low moan. Only then did Nicholas notice the boulder that weighed the beast down, trapping three of its front paws beneath it.

Nicholas didn't stop to think what he was doing. The animal was in pain, and couldn't move. He let go of Griffen's hand, and scrambled across the edge of the cliff. He slowed as he reached the beast. "Will you let me help you?" he asked.

The beast didn't even blink. It's eyes followed every move Nicholas made. Nicholas held out his hands, palms up, to show he had no weapons.

To his amazement the beast seemed to understand. It arched its neck and backed its head away from Nicholas, who took that as a sign the animal was not going to attack. Cautiously, he climbed down the rocks and tried to balance himself with his hands. He forced himself not to look down at the lake. One wrong step and he would surely die.

He reached out his hand toward the beast. His stomach turned at the thought of touching the slimy, hot hide, but he forced himself to pet it gently. Its skin was surprisingly smooth, the muscles beneath quivering at his touch. "I'll try not to hurt you," Nicholas whispered gently. He hoped the creature understood him. "I'm going to lift the rock. You'll have to move your feet away as fast as you can, because I won't be able to hold it for long."

Then he positioned himself above the boulder. If he could roll it down, gravity would pull it into the lake. Nicholas heaved his full weight against the rock. It didn't budge. He made another attempt. Still no luck. Sweat rolled down his brow, and his back felt like it was about to break. Then he noticed a long flat rock lying a little farther up the slope. He scrambled up and grabbed it.

Nicholas forced the edge of the rock under the boulder and tried to pry it up. Sure enough, it moved a little. Then he heaved the rock with all his might and it started to roll. The creature let out a mournful wail as the boulder slid over its feet. The rock hurtled down the cliff, landing in the lake with a loud splash. Lava sputtered up,

91

splattering the creature, but somehow missing Nicholas.

The creature slimed off quickly, arching its huge body into the lava. Nicholas watched amazed.

"Griffen," he called back. "We saved him!"

The creature retreated to the far side of the lava lake, and heaved its enormous bulk onto a heap of smoldering stones. Nicholas watched spellbound as it nursed its injured feet.

The beast looked up suddenly and stared at Nicholas. Then suddenly he realized the beast was trying to communicate with him.

Shifting its glance toward Griffen, the beast uncoiled its front half and shot out its forked tongue in the loremaster's direction.

Griffen staggered slightly down the hill, using his arms to steady himself. *"Lagaryth beast,"* he gasped. *"UrBeast tyrth."* He paused then continued, "Oldest *lamdethprythian-beastyth*. Father and Mother of dragon and wyrm."

"The spell, Griffen. It broke the spell! You can use your arms and speak!" Nicholas cheered.

"Still some dragonspeak." The effort to speak English seemed to exhaust Griffen.

Nicholas looked at the loremaster, then turned toward the beast. "If you can understand me, please make him all better."

The Urbeast emitted a low-pitched wail.

Nicholas watched Griffen struggle to make himself clear. "Cannot — spell strong. Magic old — not used — "

"I see — he's out of practice," Nicholas said, and to reassure the creature added, "It'll come back. You've been here a long time. I wonder how long that rock was on your foot."

"Long," Griffen said, then added with some urgency, "Speak to you he must."

"Does he know something about Berwyn?" Nicholas asked eagerly.

At the sound of the Dragon Queen's name, the Urbeast pulled back, as if stung.

"Berwyn has hurt you," Nicholas said, almost sure of it.

"Please. UrBeast talk to you. *Lythrberythladum*. Touch stone. No burn." The words seemed to stagger one by one out of Griffen's throat.

The loremaster nodded toward a small glowing stone on the right. Nicholas gulped, then looked across at the beast. Something in the creature's eyes, convinced Nicholas that it would indeed be all right to touch the smoldering rock.

Nicholas forced his hand down over the rock, and his head began to spin. The sensation grew stronger — his head felt as if it were about to burst open.

93

Then suddenly, the pressure in his head stopped. And an old, gentle voice was talking to him.

"You have saved me. I thank you. I will live as long as time. Now I will not live in pain. I do not exist outside this place. I cannot leave this pit for I am the first and last of my kind. This is my world.

"You must take that stone you now touch. It will guide you. With the stone you will see your way where all is darkness. My magic is strong, but only works beneath the earth. As you go up to the high kingdom its power will vanish."

"Can you help Griffen get his voice back?" Nicholas asked. "Without it, he'll never make music or spell the lore again."

The UrBeast paused. "I cannot give the loremaster back his voice — except for a few words. Berwyn's curse is strong."

"Berwyn!" Nicholas said, suddenly angry at the dragon queen. "She causes earthquakes, enspells Griffen and hurts you. Tell me how I can defeat her."

"No!" the UrBeast cried. "She is not to be hurt. Her wrath is just. Her egg is missing. When it is found she will become the Mother again. She will take away the curse. She is as necessary to the dragons, as I am to the heart of the earth.

"Now take the loremaster and walk upon my

back," the UrBeast instructed. "I will leave you on the other shore, and you will be able to make your way from there. I thank you again. Now you must promise me you will not reveal my presence to anyone else. Griffen has always known of me. He knows to be silent. You, too, must promise silence."

Nicholas thought this over. It would be hard not telling Ethan. The UrBeast seemed to understand but still insisted. "No one must know of me, not even your kin."

"I promise," Nicholas said aloud.

Thunder sounded inside of Nicholas's head, then contact with the beast was broken. Feeling a little dazed, Nicholas pocketed the stone and once again took Griffen's hand.

The beast uncoiled itself, and stretched its length across the lake, like a living bridge. Nicholas hesitated an instant before stepping on it, then he started across the urbeast's back. The slender body rocked like a raft, and Nicholas and Griffen made it across.

Reluctantly, Nicholas said goodbye to the UrBeast then turned to the steep, winding path ahead. Together, he and the loremaster climbed the path, following the gleam of the stone that the UrBeast had given him.

It was some time later that the stone suddenly dimmed. Nicholas's heart sank. But just as the light flickered out he felt cold, fresh air across his face. As the creature had predicted, the light would not shine outside the depths of the earth.

"We've made it, Griffen. We've come through the mountains and we're back in Nir!"

They scrambled up the slippery throat of the tunnel and through the back of an immense cavern. Before them, heaped as high as the mountain, was a pile of treasure. For a crazy moment Nicholas thought they'd come round full circle and landed back in Berwyn's lair.

And then he saw the egg — a huge oval studded with sapphires and emeralds. It lay at the back of the hoard, half-buried in the mound of treasure.

Nicholas approached it and gently touched the shell with his finger. A haze of dust blew off, making him cough.

"It's been here for ages!" Nicholas said. "Wherever *here* is."

Then he heard Ethan's voice yelling, "If you don't return the egg, you may never see Griffen again!"

"And Nicholas might be killed," Olwyn's voice added.

"I do not have this egg!" thundered a dragon who could only be Angarth. "I have never stolen from another dragon."

Griffen and Nicholas exchanged a startled glance.

Without stopping to discuss the matter, Griffen took one side of the huge jeweled egg, Nicholas the other. Together they heaved and shoved and pushed it out of the rut. Then they rolled it noisily through the narrow space between the cave wall and Angarth's hoard.

The argument was still going on when they pushed it right up under Angarth's nose. "Is this the egg in question?" Nicholas asked waving away a cloud of dust.

"Father!" Olwyn cried then threw her arms around Griffen.

"Nicholas!" exclaimed Ethan, his eyes opening very wide.

"An egg?" Angarth hissed then sat back on his haunches. All seven pairs of his eyelids snapped shut.

Olwyn smiled at Nicholas. "You saved him, but how? And where did you come from?"

"Through the tunnel in the back of Berwyn's cave." Nicholas had to bite his tongue not to give away the Urbeast's secret.

"There's a back door?" Ethan sounded very skeptical.

"Well — it wasn't quite as easy as that, but there is a passage."

"And Berwyn doesn't have it guarded?" Olwyn eyed Nicholas shrewdly.

Her father spoke up. "*Fyndtyruthurth. Berwnth.* Guarded yes. Berwyn no."

"You can speak," Olwyn cried with delight.

"Mainly in dragonspeak," Nicholas explained. "Berwyn's spell is weaker in the center of the earth for — uh — for some reason," he said evasively. "The curse was only partially lifted. He still can't spell the lore this way."

Nicholas felt Angarth's eyes upon him. "So you," Angarth said with great respect and even greater curiosity, "have been down to the earth's center and back. Interesting. Very interesting."

Meanwhile Ethan was examining the egg. "All these jewels — why this is the most beautiful object I've ever seen. Is it really an egg?"

"Yes," Angarth said grudgingly. "It is. But I haven't the foggiest idea of how it got in my hoard." He turned to Griffen. "Is it in the lore?"

"*Srythrudubnyth*. Rumor." Griffen muttered in a strangled voice. "Lore. *Nythrythyinan*. Cannot speak much."

He sounded so pitiful even Angarth looked upset.

"Can't you break the spell?" Olwyn pleaded.

Angarth looked at her with great mistrust. "Even if I could, why should I?"

Nicholas started to boil. "Listen, Angarth, haven't you caused enough trouble already? First you lie about the egg," he went on ignoring Olwyn's warning glance. "Then you won't help your supposed best friend when he's

caught in the spell of a dragon you consider your greatest enemy."

Thwack! went Angarth's tail against the base of his hoard, and the sound of tumbling metal made everyone jump. "I am always loyal to my friends," Angarth growled.

Ethan swallowed hard, and hurried to Nicholas's rescue. "But if Griffen could talk, maybe he could help you figure out what's happened here. I don't believe you stole that egg," Ethan added.

"I don't either," Olwyn said softly. "But somehow it landed in the middle of your hoard. If only my father could sing a song of seeing, maybe this mystery could be solved."

Angarth's hackles were raised and his golden scales glowed an angry red. "I cannot break Berwyn's spells. They are of as old and ancient a magic as mine, and as strong. She alone can unbind Griffen's tongue completely."

"But the egg — how will we ever know the true story?" Ethan said. "I'm sure Angarth isn't lying, and Olwyn says Berwyn isn't either. But here's the egg. There's a mystery here. We've got to solve it, or we'll all be in big trouble soon."

"Olwyn. *Crurthylaythspyth*. Truth-telling lay. Olwyn." The loremaster spoke up and pointed with his left hand to the lute on Olwyn's back. "Truth-telling lay."

100

Olwyn stared wide-eyed at her father, and slowly shook her head. "Me?" her voice trembled. "You want *me* to sing a song of seeing, and probe the past?"

He took a couple of steps toward her and reached out his hand. Gently, he brushed her tangled hair off her forehead. "Dangerous, it is," he said with great difficulty. "*Berwythurth.* Trouble, I see. But no way else."

Ethan thought a moment then said to Olwyn. "We've got no choice. Berwyn's probably back at her cave by now. She's going to find out Griffen and Nicholas have escaped. It won't take her long to trail them here. She's going to see that egg, then POW!" Ethan shot his fist into the air.

Even Angarth looked up. The light in his eyes looked dim and faded. Nicholas caught his glance and thought of the poor UrBeast in the cavern's below. Angarth was ancient too, even by dragon standards. Suddenly Nicholas was inspired. "Angarth, maybe you've just forgotten what's going on."

Angarth growled low in his throat. "A dragon never forgets."

"Ah," Nicholas contradicted gently, "not usually. But a dragon who has had such a long and rich and full life, with so many adventures — "

Ethan caught Nicholas's drift. "And so much

treasure. Why the hoard of Angarth is rumored to be the greatest in the Seven Kingdoms." Ethan noticed Angarth didn't look very pleased and turned toward Griffen to support him. "According to the lore — right?"

Griffen nodded cautiously.

"But I tell the truth. I have never stolen an egg." This time Angarth sounded a little less sure of himself.

Olwyn looked up, then took a deep breath. She picked up her lute and faced Angarth head on. "I do feel you're telling the truth — but that Berwyn is too. May I at least try to solve this puzzle?"

Angarth was silent for what felt like forever. Finally he gave his scales a shake and moved creakily toward the front of the cave. There he circled round and round like a cat, and settled down jangling and creaking in a heap. His massive bulk curled protectively around the jewelled egg. "You may sing, Olwyn. I have indeed done and seen many things. Perhaps there is something — a small insignificant thing — I have forgotten."

Olwyn motioned for the others to move closer to her. Then picking up her lute she strummed a series of haunting minor chords.

She began to hum softly. The sung tale was long and rambling and hard for Ethan to follow. Then suddenly the music changed, and

Ethan realized he was *seeing* what Olwyn was singing and not just hearing it.

There was no camera, no movie screen, no VCR, but the cavern was filled with a three-dimensional picture. A high mountain peak, jagged and snowcapped towered against a blue sky. Creatures that were not dragons soared below the summit.

"Pterodactyls!" Nicholas cried and Ethan knew he hadn't been seeing things. Whenever this story was set, it was long enough ago for there to be dinosaurs roaming the earth. Dinosaurs — *and* dragons.

Griffen clapped his left hand over Nicholas's mouth. "No speak. Dangerous. Olwyn," he said fearfully.

Nicholas swallowed hard and glanced at Olwyn. The girl was in a trance. The vision in the cave seemed to shimmer and fade. Olwyn moaned a little, then returned to her song, her voice weak and thin at first, then slowly growing stronger.

As her voice strengthened the picture in the air sharpened into focus. There was a swirl of mist, then the image of a mountain peak like the one near Berwyn's lair. A golden winged figure flew into view. It hovered above the peak, just as one of the Pterodactyls dipped down.

"Angarth," Ethan whispered under his

breath. "He was there."

Nicholas nodded in the dim light of the cave. He watched the image waver a little, then he saw the jeweled egg perched right on the edge of a cliff. The entrance to Berwyn's lair was nowhere in sight.

The Pterodactyl hovered over the egg. Nicholas caught his breath. The airborne dinosaur was about to claim it for its breakfast. It dove down toward the egg but somehow missed its target. The beat of its wings sent the egg right over the edge of the cliff! There was another flash of gold. Suddenly, there was Angarth, slimmer, more golden, and not quite as huge as he was now, holding the egg in his massive jaw. His eyes glinted greedily as he viewed his jeweled prize.

"Oh, no!" Angarth's wail broke the spell, and Olwyn collapsed. "I remember now. I thought it was just a pretty gem. I'd never seen an egg up close before." He sounded very apologetic.

Nicholas rushed up to Olwyn, and reached for his pack. He grabbed the waterskin, and sprinkled a few drops on her face. She opened her eyes, and blinked. "I'm all right," she said hoarsely. "Everything will be all right now."

Nicholas breathed a sigh of relief and sat back on his heels.

Ethan turned to Angarth. "So that's that," he said, hooking his thumbs in his belt loops.

"You can just bring the egg back to Berwyn and — "

Angarth's hackles rose. "I will do no such thing."

Griffen struggled to speak. "Must sorry say. Must. War must not be. *Nievyrthyrdindath!*"

"Quiet!" commanded Angarth. "I am king among dragons. I will not be called a thief when, in fact, I saved the egg." The thought apparently had just occurred to him, and obviously pleased him very much. "I am, a hero — a dragon hero. Berwyn should thank me for not letting her precious egg be eaten."

Ethan rolled his eyes as Angarth puffed out his chest and strutted toward the entrance to the lair.

At that very moment, the mountain started to shake, and a loud bellow filled the sky.

"Berwyn!" Olwyn cried. "She's back. And she knows you've escaped."

"I wonder what took her so long," Nicholas grumbled.

Just then Ethan noticed the egg. The earth trembled again. This time the egg rolled out of the cavern, between Angarth's hind legs, through the opening and onto the ledge beyond. It rattled into a natural hollow in the middle of the clearing.

"The egg!" Ethan gasped.

"My egg!" Berwyn bellowed. "You have had

it all along. You thief. You liar. You attacker of unborn dragons."

With that Berwyn spread her wings and plunged toward Angarth. The dragon king was too startled to move. "How did you get through my spell?" he wondered aloud. But she attacked with the full force of her fury, sending forth a river of white hot fire.

Eleven

Battle Cry

"Stop!" Olwyn cried, a newfound power in her voice. Surviving the song of seeing had somehow lent her strength. "Look." She pointed to the sky.

All eyes followed her upraised hand. There, forming an almost perfect vee against the scarlet sunset, flew seven dragons. They were headed straight for Angarth's mountain.

Angarth recognized them at once. "The envoy from the moot," he said, then called a welcome. To the boys' surprise Berwyn swallowed her own fire, and actually joined in the greeting.

"Now jussstice will be done," she hissed.

Nicholas stared in wonder as the seven dragons landed. Three were bejeweled like Berwyn, but their coloring was a dusky greenish-grey. The other dragons had jewel-like coloring: one peacock blue, one sunshine yellow, another a deep earthy red and one a purple sort of green.

Nicholas was sure that, like birds, the brightly-colored ones were the males.

"Fingal!" Ethan waved to his friend. "You've come from the moot!" He noticed that Fingal didn't look very happy at all.

The six other messenger dragons turned to Fingal. The young beast swallowed hard, and took a step toward the center of the clearing. "Mighty Angarth, Majestic Berwyn: The moot has taken its vote."

"And of coursssse I have won. Here'ss proof possssitive," said Berwyn, and pointed to the egg which was now tucked under Angarth's wing. "It was in his hoard all along. He cannot deny it."

"I do not deny it," Angarth said with great dignity. "I have learned from a song of seeing that I did take your egg." The three female messenger dragons hissed knowingly. "But I did not steal it," he went on. "I saved it. You left it unprotected on a ledge. I found it just as it was about to roll down the side of the mountain and break. Splat," he concluded taking great delight in the word. He liked it so much he said it again, mimicking Berwyn's hiss. "Sssssplat."

Berwyn gasped and ribbons of colorful steam poured out of her nostrils and ears. "Liar," she accused. "Shame of all dragons who have ever lived. I — will *rumartyhy tyringla*— I — will *artmathyn lyrdyn garaborynthal —* "

Nicholas expected her to blast Angarth then and there. But he soon realized she was afraid of hurting her egg. She wouldn't attack Angarth as long as he hovered near the egg. Nicholas smiled grimly. He wondered if Angarth realized this too. The old dragon hadn't lived to such a great age by taking unnecessary chances.

Berwyn glared a moment at Angarth, then turned toward the messengers and said, "But we have not heard how the moot voted."

Fingal hemmed and hawed, and his eyes began whirling nervously in different directions. "The vote was split," he began hesitantly. "Half the dragons voted that Angarth was not a thief and half voted that he was. We cannot risk a dragon war over this feud. You must settle this matter between yourselves. No matter who wins or loses, the dragons will not speak of this again. It will be erased from the lore."

Berwyn contained her rage for half a second, and then hurled herself toward Fingal. The young dragon squawked and stumbled backward over the edge of the cliff.

"Fingal!" Ethan and Nicholas cried. They dashed toward the edge to see Fingal falling into the valley below. Fortunately, he remembered to flap his wings. In seconds he regained

109

his balance and headed skywards — *away* from Angarth's lair. The other messengers mumbled polite good-byes in dragonspeak and took off before Berwyn had another chance to vent her anger.

For a moment the boys forgot all about Berwyn, Angarth and the egg. They stared after Fingal until he was only a purple streak across the sunset. "We may never see him again," Ethan said.

"Get back — toward the cave," Olwyn's warning suddenly echoed across the narrow clearing.

Nicholas whirled around. To his horror, Berwyn had taken to the sky. She was circling Angarth's lair, lacing the air with fire. Beneath her, the golden dragon was waving his long neck back and forth, periodically throwing back his head and sounding an earsplitting cry.

Nicholas wasn't sure what all this meant, but it didn't look good. Shoving Ethan in front of him, he dived for the base of the cliff where Olwyn was already crouched next to her father. Oddly, Griffen was humming, and a moment later Olwyn joined in. Neither boy paid much attention to the song. Their attention was riveted to the fiery drama in the sky.

Angarth was obviously the more powerful of the two dragons, and Ethan was sure he was also more cunning. The dragon king tilted his gilded body at an angle to the setting sun, and the brilliant flash of light temporarily blinded Berwyn. He shot a tongue of fire at her, and she roared in pain as it scorched the soft skin of her underside, but recovered swiftly and darted across his path. He wheeled his huge bulk around, his wings pumping furiously, but Berwyn was too fast for him. She circled around and attacked him from the rear, blasting him with a scalding stream of steam and smoke.

The king dragon shrieked with pain, and Olwyn buried her head in her arms and let out a moan. Griffen nudged her hard again. "Hum," he said.

Olwyn shook her head, her voice ragged. "They'll fight to the death."

Griffen stood up, and alone he began to hum. He grasped Nicholas's shoulder and shook him.

Nicholas stared blankly at the Loremaster, then understood. He swallowed the sobs rising in his throat and lent his voice to Griffen's song. He couldn't imagine what good humming would do, but it was better than crouching on the sidelines and doing nothing.

At first Ethan thought the noise he heard came from behind him, from his brother and Griffen. Then he realized there was another noise that came from the center of the clearing. While the others watched the dragons, Ethan's eyes were fixed on the egg. The longer he

watched the sparkly object, the more he was sure the sound came from the egg. "That's funny," he mused aloud.

A second later, he leapt to his feet and bolted right up to the egg.

"It's hatching. It's hatching!" he shouted. A shower of sparks was still falling from the sky. He shielded his eyes and fell to his knees. By this time the egg was shaking violently, and its sound was as loud as thunder in his ear.

The sparks stopped, and the ledge shook as Berwyn landed with a crash. She stumbled over to the egg, nudged it with her snout, and let out a high crooning sound. Then she began pecking at the egg with a bony growth that jutted out from beneath her chin.

Angarth circled the clearing and peered down at the scene below. "It's hatching!" Nicholas cupped his hands and yelled up. "There's going to be a new dragon!"

Angarth snorted, and slowly descended, landing on top of his cave. "A new dragon?" He ruffled his wings, and craned his neck to get a better view.

"A new dragon is a very important thing," he said, though no one was listening. "That is why I kept the egg safe all these years."

Holding her father's hand, Olwyn had crept up beside him. "The humming helped this happen. Dragons hum their hatchlings to birth."

She turned to her father, her eyes brimming. "I have so much to learn," she whispered. "I know so little lore."

Berwyn wrenched her eyes away from the egg and gazed at Griffen. "Loremaster of Nir, without your lore, my dragonling would not have hatched. I was too busy fighting to remember to hum the egg open. Thus, I will lift forever the Curse of Peredur from your lips. You will speak and sing again — perhaps more beautifully and truthfully than before."

Griffen stood still a moment, as if he couldn't quite believe his ears. "The curse is lifted?" he asked, but the fact he could speak again was enough of an answer. He bowed low before Berwyn. "Thank you, Dragon Queen."

At that very moment a small hooked beak dripping its yellow yolky substance poked out.

The shell parted and out tumbled a damp, bedraggled creature. It was brown, with an enormous head, and extraordinarily large pink eyes that blinked furiously in the sun.

The head swiveled on a limp scrawny neck, until it laid eyes on Berwyn. Then the baby dragon let out a high-pitched squawk. Nicholas watched, grinning, as it staggered in its mother's direction then fell in a heap at her feet.

Berwyn's scales turned a rosy hue and she nudged the hatchling with her nose.

"So now the battle is ended and peace can begin." Griffen's voice made everyone look up.

"Nothing is ended," fumed Berwyn.

"Not until I am told I am not a thief," Angarth added, equally stubborn.

Olwyn blew her hair out of her eyes and stalked up to Berwyn. "Say it. Say it now. There are few enough dragons in the world. You can't afford to fight amongst yourselves."

Berwyn sat silent as a stone.

Then Ethan, still crouched near the hatchling's shell, spoke up. "Angarth can't be a thief anymore," he said reasonably. "There *is* no egg."

Nicholas looked at his brother with great respect. "Brainwave's right," he said, helping the younger boy to his feet. "The egg is gone, the hatchling is born. Like the dragon envoy said: It will be erased from the lore."

Berwyn peered down at her hatchling. "I am grateful he has survived."

Griffen coughed. Angarth scowled at him, but then turned toward Berwyn. "You have my apology. I was honestly mistaken. I thought the egg was a jewel — you lay such beautiful eggs."

Berwyn's scales rustled with pleasure. "Yesssss. My eggsssss are lovely, but not as lovely as my dragonling. And I will no longer think of Angarth as a thief. You have been a hero. I will tell the young one as he growssss about the mighty Angarth, the Golden One, who sssaved him."

Nicholas shivered in a blast of wind and looked up into the sky. "It's dark, and look — the stars are rising over the horizon."

The dragonling looked up. It let out a gurgle and started toward the edge of the cliff. Berwyn scooped it back. She made a puzzled crooning sort of sound. "Star?" she repeated.

"See," Nicholas pointed to where the sun had set. There was a rim of greenish light and above that a twinkling star.

"That's no star," said Berwyn in a tone of disgust. "Stars don't rise in the west."

The dragonling peeked out from under her wing at the sky and let out an excited gurgle.

"What's he so happy about?" Olwyn asked.

"I'm almost afraid to find out!" Ethan commented, "But look, that star is coming straight out of the Valley of the Lost Dragon!"

Twelve

Bangles and Bones

Berywn was right. The gleam over the western horizon wasn't a star, after all. As it came closer it became clear that it was a young dragon. Cautiously, the creature circled the group on the ledge below. It let out one wary cry, then landed.

"You again," Angarth muttered. He definitely did not sound pleased to see Fingal. "You have caused much trouble."

"No, he hasn't," Griffen spoke up quickly in the young dragon's defense. "He brought the boys here. Without Fingal, Nicholas and Olwyn would never have found me." Turning quickly to Berwyn, Griffen added, "And we never would have solved the mystery of the egg."

Berwyn looked up from the egg. Her pearly eyes actually misted over. "I would have losssst my hatchling," she hissed in a tender voice. She nodded toward the boys. "How can I thank you?"

117

"By letting me take them home now, as I promised." Fingal's answer surprised everyone. "They have a mother and father who worry about them — as you worry about Grymp."

"Grymp?" several voices repeated at once.

"How do you know itsssss name?" Berwyn snapped peevishly.

"He told me when I flew in," Fingal said bursting with pride. "He announced himself as Grymp, son of Berwyn, daughter of — "

Berwyn jealously reached out and gathered her hatchling under her wings. "Ssssooo," she said, still determined to ignore Fingal. "Humans have mothers, too." She peered long and hard at the boys. "Then I will give you a gift for your mother."

To their surprise, Berwyn craned her neck and preened the scales just below her wing. She straightened up and dropped a gem at Nicholas's feet.

He questioned her with a look. At her nod he picked it up. "This is beautiful. Thank you." He opened his palm and showed Ethan a cameo pendant. The white ivory was delicately carved in the form of a female dragon encrusted with tiny jewels. She looked a lot like Berwyn.

"Mom will love it. And we needed to buy her a present too," Ethan said.

"But what about Dad?" Nicholas gave Ethan

a worried look. "If we're late getting back, the store will be closed."

"Your father shall have a gift, too," Angarth said a bit pompously. He shuffled back into the cave. There was a loud crash followed by a series of dragon curses. When Angarth emerged a few moments later he was carrying a long narrow rock between his teeth.

"Ethan told me your father likes to study bones. Here are bones of one of the lost ones." The dragon dropped the stone on the ground.

"It's a fossil," Ethan declared, amazed. The rock was no ordinary fossil — captured in its surface was the complete, perfect skeleton of a tiny, lizard-sized dinosaur. "He'll love it!" Ethan beamed. "This time I even feel a bit like a hero," he said.

"Except we haven't found the king, yet," Nicholas reminded him.

"But we have," Griffen and Angarth said at once.

Griffen went on to explain. "He's not far from here, in the caves behind the heights of Peredur. He is quite comfortable, with a small court of followers."

"We were on our way there, when all the trouble started," Angarth added.

Berwyn warned Angarth off with a hiss.

"But perhaps Berwyn can help bring him back here," Angarth said in a chivalrous tone.

"So our adventures are all over," said Ethan, trying not to sound too disappointed.

"Oh, I wouldn't be so quick to say that," Nicholas warned. "Particularly when Dad turns up outside the store in Frenchman's Bay and we're not there."

"But you will be," Fingal said. "If Angarth will help me, I can get you back to the borders of your time within the hour."

Nicholas didn't move. He stared sadly at Olwyn and Griffen. "I hope we'll run into each other again."

Griffen stood up and hugged him, then opened his arms wider and Ethan ran up to be hugged, too. "There will always be a place for you in the Seven Kingdoms," the loremaster promised warmly.

"Until next time," Olwyn said, hating good-byes as much as Nicholas. "Don't worry," she chuckled, "I'll call you next time trouble's brewing around here — if Fingal doesn't beat me to it."

"How'd you know?" Ethan questioned. "Fingal told us not to tell you — "

"Oh, I figured it out. Fingal's the one dragon I've met who loves to break all the rules. Besides, only dragons guard the entrances between worlds. Someone had to let you in, you know."

Nicholas settled himself between Angarth's

massive wings. Ethan, being smaller, rode on Fingal's back. Angarth led the way, not across the mountains, or over the Valley of the Lost Dragon, but up and up and up — heading straight for the heart of the moon.

Nicholas heard a whooshing sound and suddenly he felt lightheaded. He closed his eyes for a moment as he felt something shake and then thump.

"Hey, watch it," he called to Angarth. His eyes popped open, and he blinked. There were bright, colored lights and the familiar sounds of honking horns, Christmas carols and the tolling of a bell.

"Nicholas, we're back," Ethan said sadly. "Where are you?"

"Here," Nicholas said, sounding equally glum. It took a moment to recognize his surroundings. They were at the stop of a quaint street that curved up the hill from Frenchman's Bay.

"Look," Ethan cried. He pulled one hand out of his pocket and started waving. Slowly making its way up the block was the Lord's van. "There's Dad."

"Ethan," Nicholas dropped his voice to a whisper. "We've landed in the right place." He pointed to the sign that creaked above the shop behind them. *Bangles and Bones* it said in fancy letters.

"Hi, boys," Thomas Lord called. He was a tall man, with thinning dark hair, blue eyes and a friendly smile. "Sorry I'm late, but Arnie had trouble with his truck and we had to go to the service station."

"You're late?" Ethan couldn't believe their luck.

"You're late." Nicholas repeated and started to laugh. "And *we* were worried we wouldn't get here in time."

His father looked at him puzzled. "In time? You've been gone for hours."

Ethan giggled. "You know how it is at Christmas. We kept looking in all the shops."

His stepfather gave him a funny look as they got into the van. "All *three* shops? I guess time passes differently when you're a kid," he said, as he backed into a driveway and made a U-turn down the narrow, winding street. "So did you get your shopping done? And did you get a chance to check out Bangles and Bones?"

Ethan glanced at Nicholas. "Bangles and Bones."

Nicholas grinned, then felt around in his back pack. The sharp outline of the fossil was still there. He hadn't forgotten it.

Ethan poked Nicholas in the arm and uncurled his palm. There, glinting like a dragon's tooth in the moonlight was the cameo for their mom.

"Don't ask too many questions, Dad," Nicholas teased. "Let's just say we had a very interesting time looking for your present."

"And Mom's too," Ethan added as Mr. Lord drove down the road leading out of town. "We really lucked out."

"Blame your luck on that," Thomas Lord suddenly said, pulling onto an overlook above the bay. He pointed east where a full moon hung over the water. As they watched, two clouds streaked in front of it. The clouds were of a familiar shape — silhouettes of creatures with long necks and spiny ridges and wings.

"Dragon clouds over the moon," Thomas Lord mused dreamily, then laughed. "That's what I used to call them when I was your age, Nicholas."

"Dragon clouds?" Nicholas tried to sound scornful. "Aw, dragons are just kid stuff."

Ethan gasped, and Nicholas elbowed him hard. He put a finger to his lips and pointed out the window. The clouds over the horizon had turned around, and seemed to be facing them. Then just as Mr. Lord revved up the engine and headed out of the overlook, a distant keening filled the air.

"Goodbye," Ethan whispered, kneeling on the back seat and keeping one eye on the dark, starry sky.